PRAISE FOR
LIA MATERA
AND
WHERE LAWYERS FEAR TO TREAD

"Funny, clear-eyed and strong."
Robert B. Parker

"A right snappy storyteller."
Gregory Mcdonald

"Willa Jansson is a delightful narrator."
Drood Review

"[An] exceptional debut ... A delightful romp, and a satiric and satisfying look at the training grounds for the legal profession."
Wilson Library Bulletin

"If Civil Procedure, Evidence or Remedies aren't enough to keep you busy, here's a suggestion: read Lia Matera's new murder mystery. . . . A fun read."
Hastings Law News

WHERE LAWYERS FEAR TO TREAD

Lia Matera

BALLANTINE BOOKS • NEW YORK

The law school and law firms depicted in this book are imaginary. So are the lawyers, professors, and law students. Any resemblance they bear to real people and institutions is entirely coincidental. San Francisco, Stanford University, and Ronald Reagan, all used here fictitiously, are not imaginary. Neither is the résumé madness of law students.

ISBN 0-345-37125-9

Manufactured in the United States of America

First Ballantine Books Edition: June 1991

To the editors of the *Hastings Constitutional Law Quarterly*, Volume 8, for letting me boss them around.

LAW SCHOOLS DON'T have football teams, they have law reviews. Law reviews may look like large paperbacks, but they are arenas. Legal scholars maul each other in polite footnotes, students scrimmage and connive for editorial positions, and the intellectual bloodlust of law professors is appeased, rah rah.

Law reviews are edited by law students. After three years of competing for grades, jobs, even vending machine food (it's nothing but Fig Newtons after four o'clock), law students will do anything—if it means someone else doesn't get to do it.

"Top ten percent and law review," that's the magic phrase. If you don't want to work in Puyallup, Washington, or Lawton, Oklahoma, if you want to work in a big city law firm, if you want a decent salary, if you want a job in a government agency or a hip organization like the American Civil Liberties Union, you'd better be in the top ten percent of your class, and you'd better be on law review. And if you're not at Harvard, Yale, or Stanford Law, it's best to be editor-in-chief.

I was editor-in-chief of a law review for a while, through

no fault of my own. I replaced an infinitely more qualified woman named Susan Green.

Here's everything I know about Susan Green, former editor-in-chief of the *Malhousie Law Review*:

Susan Green was born to Dr. Sidney and Mrs. Greta Green in 1960, the year I, Willa Jansson, started grade school. While I played with incense sticks and chose my mantra at one of the first alternative schools in San Francisco, Susan Green, super-baby, learned her alphabet from flashcards displayed by an overqualified nanny. While I was hating my first job, washing dishes at a vegetarian restaurant, Susan Green was giving piano recitals and taking ballet lessons. While I organized high school antiwar rallies and refused to salute the flag, Susan Green began using her eidetic memory to memorize patriotic verse. When my parents joined the Peace Corps, Dr. and Mrs. Green began their retirement cruise, leaving Susan in an elegant boarding school in Washington, D.C. So, when I hitchhiked there to join fifteen thousand or so others camped around the White House, Susan Green and I were in the same city for the first time in our lives.

That didn't happen again for four years, when we both ended up at Stanford University, me after much impecunious gypsying around the country (which did not affect my college entrance exam score), and she after graduating with honors from the toughest of prep schools. Not only did we end up at the same university at the same time, but our families actually met at freshman orientation. My father looked faded and ill after two years of diarrhea in Liberia, but my mother was still rosy and pear-shaped under twenty pounds of African jewelry. Susan's parents looked made-for-TV and smelled faintly of leather from their new Jaguar. We all ended up at the same little outdoor picnic table for a cafeteria lunch. Two students at the next table were discussing their rapes, and Mrs. Green went white and whispered to my mother that she wished they *wouldn't*.

"I've been raped myself," my mother said in her squeaky, carrying voice. "Twice. And it really is therapeutic to talk about it."

There was a shocked silence. Mrs. Green clutched her fur collar, sidling closer to her pinch-lipped husband.

My mother, characteristically unaware of having given offense, thus noticed the band of endangered wildlife around Mrs. Green's neck. I knew what was coming. I'd already gotten the "Love animals—don't eat them or wear them" lecture once that morning, when I'd ordered a cheeseburger.

So when Mother piously intoned, "Love animals—" I did Mrs. Green a favor. I cut in, "—they're delicious."

My father laughed, but no one else did. The Greens took a few more hasty bites of salad, then fled.

Susan Green and I had one class together that year, and I wrote her off as a walking résumé, an amalgam of dull accomplishments in an impeccably preppy shell, the kind of girl who wore a pearl necklace to class and paid two dollars a bar for Neutrogena soap so her cheeks would be as shiny as the rest of the sorority's. (Her sorority motto was "Learn from the successful and inspire the unfortunate"; luckily, inspiration is cheap.)

In spite of myself, I had to admire Susan's brainpower. She had total recall, a photographic memory. And she spoke in well-edited paragraphs, complete with topic sentence, supporting facts, and brief restatement. She was long on information and short on insight, whereas I have the kind of sloppy brain that hares off on romantic associations and refuses to memorize.

I had a few more classes with Susan along the way, never did as well on the exams, never impressed my professors, and got into a lot of trouble over some articles I wrote for the school paper (I called Leland Stanford a bloodsucking pirate, which I learned was not beyond dispute, after all).

Then the fates decreed that Susan Green and I begin law school together, make law review together, and end up on the editorial board together.

But here's one thing we didn't do together: the day I argued with Larry Tchielowicz about the war in Vietnam, somebody smashed Susan's head in as she bent over a manuscript.

2

"Look what the Communists have done to Vietnam—too bad you radicals didn't keep quiet and let Nixon win the war."

There were half a dozen other editors in the law review

office, sleepily filling their cups with metallic wastewater from the coffee urn. They regarded Tchielowicz with weary incredulity. Exams were less than four weeks away; only I could be goaded into fighting the old battles.

"You'd have protested too if the government planned to kill your ass on foreign soil." Tchielowicz was five or six years younger than me; he'd been just a kid during those years of division, death, and defoliation.

"No Republicans in foxholes?" Tchielowicz's thin lips—the only thin part of the muscle-bound, big-headed man—twitched back a smile. "The army's paying my way through law school, I'll have you know. Paid my way through college, too. I've already done basic training, and I owe them six more years, after the bar exam." He rubbed his smallish, bent nose. "So you see, I've already consented to let the government do with my ass what it will."

I treated Tchielowicz to my candid opinion of this arrangement.

Susan Green rapped at the glass of the inner office to try to shut me up. She'd talked the law school into erecting a plywood and acrylic enclosure around the half dozen desks in the basement office, separating them from the sagging Naugahyde couches and encrusted coffee accoutrements. The partitions created an illusion of privacy, but they stopped several feet short of the ceiling to allow for a maze of overhead pipes, and they barely muffled the sound of conversation on the other side.

Since it took sixteen of us to do the proofreading, disparaging, and kvetching known as the editorial process, and since most of us did it in the outer office, Susan's inner sanctum was less than silent at the best of times. But I honored her request by concluding more quietly, and more kindly, that Tchielowicz was a prostitute for the crypto-fascist war machine.

Before Tchielowicz could respond, Jake Whittsen strolled in and ruffled my hair—I don't know why men treat small blond women like puppies. "Are you coming to hear Jane Day?" Even Jake's voice was gorgeous, about an octave lower than most men's, and so quiet it sounded like pillowtalk no matter what he said.

Jane Day was one of those damned Republican feminists. You know, Get women out of the home and into the Mercedes for luncheon with the Ladies Against Drug Abuse ("Madame Chairman, I'd like to propose a toast to the eradication of drug use").

She belonged to every bar association committee ever devised; it was spooky how often you ran across her name in bar publications. She was currently on the rubber chicken circuit, trying to win her party's nomination for state attorney general. The law school, which happened to be her alma mater, was hosting a reception for her that afternoon. The editorial board of the law review had been invited; the rest of the student body was not deemed worthy to break bread with our distinguished professors.

I was inclined to go with Jake—it was a chance to sit beside him and become intoxicated by his cologne (probably selected by his stunning and sophisticated wife, alas).

But Tchielowicz remarked that he guessed Jane Fonda was too busy building up her pectorals to worry about the Vietnamese people now that they were being slaughtered by socialists instead of capitalists, and I couldn't leave the fray. I declined Jake's invitation.

A few students drifted in, earnestly discussing the relative merits of squash and raquetball. They drank the dregs of the coffee, then Reeboked off to a commercial paper class. Professor Haas, a comparative law professor with a lilting Swedish accent and a shy, charming smile, came in to get the latest issue of the review, hot off the presses and stacked on the floor near Susan's desk. Professor Miles, who'd been teaching trusts and wills long before they'd mummified her, stalked in clutching a copy. Through the plywood partition, I heard her shriek to Susan that we'd failed to list all her degrees in the editor's note preceding her article on blind trusts.

That was the last thing I ever heard anyone say to Susan Green.

I left to go to my federal income tax class. I didn't particularly want to go, but I was beginning to suspect Larry Tchielowicz thought I was cute when I was mad.

And while my tax professor lasciviously discussed his favorite tax shelters, someone stood behind Susan Green, raised up a weapon, and brought it down twice on the back of her head.

3

JOHN HANCOCK HENDERSON, a several-times-removed descendant of the guy with the big loopy signature, hovered over my desk. The look on his face bespoke a great tightness of the nether parts.

"The masthead shows a clear pattern of ascension," he spat, as though we'd been arguing about it.

"Like Jacob's ladder?"

"It goes: editor-in-chief on top, then next row, executive editor on the left and senior articles editor on the right."

"So I sit at the right hand of the Lord?"

"No! Well, yes, but the fact that executive editor is positioned first in the row indicates that it's next in importance to editor-in-chief."

"I hope all that fits on your résumé."

Henderson was looking excessively crabby, even for him. He was of middle height, getting plumper every year, with a complexion that spotted around finals time, and a big face with big features (Mary West called him Mr. Potato Head). "I know what you're thinking, that this is somehow in bad taste. But this law review has been in existence eighty-eight years, and we have an obligation to carry on! There's no excuse for getting behind''—he said the word with sincere horror—''so we've got to determine who's in charge.''

''Nobody needs to be in charge! I'll do final edits for style and substance, you keep doing the final technical edits, and we'll set the deadlines between us. The only executive decision left for Susan was choosing the articles for the summer issue. The other three issues are either at the printer's or almost ready to go!''

What I didn't say was that there would be a mass revolt of editors if John Henderson started cracking the whip. Susan had spent half her time mollifying John's underling technical editors to keep them from mutiny. He was a good technical editor—he could spot a spacing error in a footnote from a hundred yards—but that was about all you could say for him as a human being.

Anyway, the conversation seemed ghoulish.

''Go be monomaniacal elsewhere, would you, Henderson? I have to finish reading this case before my trusts class.''

Mary West came in, looking like a refugee from a *True Sex* article on ''Why Leather Makes Me Hot.''

Mary had waist-length black hair and a figure that made her pale, lantern-jawed face beside the point. She had a habit of lacing her fingers behind her head to show off a bustline that needed no fanfare. She also liked to spend money she didn't have—hence the tight leather pants and high-heeled Italian boots—and to bed first-year students who didn't know any better.

I'll say this for Mary, she didn't mince her words. "Masturbating over the masthead again, John?"

He flushed pink as an oiled pig and left the inner office, shouting, "I'll take this up with our faculty advisor, thank you!"

Mary sauntered over to Susan's desk, which had been emptied of effects by the police and scrubbed clean by me. (John had delegated the task to the janitor in a chillingly seigneural way, so I'd felt obliged to do it myself.)

"Christ, who'd want to bash Cotton Panties? Clean, white, and practical"—that had been Mary's assessment of Susan.

I have very long, blond bangs. If I tuck my chin down I can examine the gray streak that is developing on the right side. I did that.

"You don't suppose John killed Susan so he could be the Big Footnote?" She smiled her I've-seen-it-all smile. "What's this shit about him going to the faculty? They're not going to make him e-in-c are they?"

I shook my head. John and I had had many dealings with the faculty. I had recognized their pomposity and worked around it; John had met them with equal pomposity, which they seemed to find disrespectful. If our faculty had to choose a replacement for Susan, it wouldn't be John.

"Damn him!" I flared. "If he gets me made e-in-c, I'll kill him!"

Mary raised what was left of her carefully tweezed and feathered brows.

4

I RAN UP the terraced aisle to the back of the amphitheater-shaped classroom and slid into the seat beside Harold Scharr. Harold is one of those lean European types, with a thin, attentive face, hair like black silk, and expressive eyes that abet a wicked tongue. He turned and flashed his white teeth at me.

Professor Miles called us to order with the words "sale of trust assets." She assumed her characteristic stance: feet, in black pumps, wide apart; hips thrust forward, skinny arms akimbo. She scanned the aisles. I had a feeling she was gunning for me.

"Ms. Willa Jansson." She said my name dryly. "*Palvers* v. *Executor*."

I opened my casebook, propped it upright on my desk as though I meant to refer to it. Then I flipped through the illicit, prefab case outlines used by most law students. I read the bold-print caption aloud: "Attorney for Trustor's survivor may not bid on Trust assets auctioned to pay costs." I nearly added, *So there*.

"Costs of executing the Trust only, of course." A flat statement.

I skimmed the outline; that was all the case said, but I knew there must be a catch. I took a guess. "The State Bar Canons of Legal Ethics prohibit lawyers from bidding on their clients' property at any judicial or foreclosure sale, regardless of the expense to be defrayed. Otherwise, lawyers could run up litigation costs, hoping to buy their clients' property at quick-sale prices."

Harold murmured, "What's wrong with a little free enterprise?"

I didn't realize that this obscure point of ethics would turn out to be one of the most baffling aspects of Susan Green's murder.

After class I was dying for a cup of coffee; the stuff was mother's milk to me since I'd quit smoking. Harold and I were pushing toward the cafeteria (fifteen hundred of us sardined into one downtown building: Malhousie's brochures called it "cozy collegiality"). We were speculating about Professor Miles' obvious displeasure at my correct answer, when Dean Sorenson, about seven feet tall and weighing less than a broomstick, wrapped his simian fingers around my arm and shouted over the din, "Ms. Jansson, a moment of your time."

Harold melted away like snow on a warm turd.

"I've been talking to John Henderson." To give the dean credit, he didn't sound happy about it. "I'd like to know how the other members of law review feel about the appointment of a new editor."

A rushing student bumped me up against the dean, nearly turning a corridor full of cozy colleagues into dominoes. "Late to contracts," he called over his shoulder; first-year students are pathologically punctual.

I shouted to the dean, "I don't think we need anyone to fill in for Susan at this point."

Dean Sorenson's gaunt face seemed to lengthen when he raised his black brows. He tried to look mournful and managed to look insincere. "Susan was one of the finest young women I've ever been privileged to meet."

"Me, too." I hated blocking an aisle of foot traffic to talk about how fine Susan Green had been, but the dean showed no willingness to move along.

"I understand you and the other editors have talked to the police detectives?"

"That's right." I hoped my face didn't reveal the contempt I'd felt for the homicide "inspectors," with their transparently trick questions.

"You, uh, didn't see anything?"

I shook my head.

He frowned and stuck out his lower lip (Harold Scharr does a classic imitation of this). I was beginning to feel like a butterfly pinned to cardboard—without a quick shot of caffeine, I was going to die.

"Well, well. About this other business. Mr. Henderson seems to think you'd better have a new editor. But I wouldn't want to do anything by fiat. What say the editors elect a new chief? Sound fair?"

What could I say?

I found a quorum of editors having lunch in the basement office.

John Henderson had his back to me. He had a copy of the law review open to the masthead, and he was declaiming, "I think it's clear!"

The more polite editors were stifling their laughter.

I was in too rotten a mood to be tactful. "Jesus, Henderson, it's one goddam line on your résumé! Is there any humiliation you wouldn't endure for a few extra grand a year?"

John whirled to face me, and Tchielowicz boomed from the corner, "Senior articles editor is the number two position. Willa should be editor-in-chief, if anyone."

"Oh turn it off, Tchielowicz." I pushed past John. I found my cup and filled it with sludge from the urn. "The dean says we have to have a goddam election."

Henderson actually blanched. "I told him I was next in line of succession."

"You and Richard the Second." Mary West was sitting on Jake Whittsen's lap. Mary never did sit on a chair if there was a man's lap to be had. No one even noticed anymore. "Let's make it easy. I nominate Willa."

Tchielowicz seconded, and I was saying, "I won't be railroaded—" as the voice vote did just that.

"You dimbulb!" I complained to a livid John Henderson. "Are you satisfied?"

He catapulted out of the office, tossing the law review onto the floor.

Tchielowicz began to hum "For He's a Jolly Good Fellow," and I advised him to shut up before he attracted a female moose. "The masthead stays the same. You guys can call me whatever you want—" There were a few hoots and suggestions from the audience.

Mary said, "Do I get to be senior articles editor now?"

"Nice try." We kept Mary around because she was funny as hell, but a lazier editor never lived.

I looked at "my staff" over the rim of my coffee cup.

Susan had gotten the overworked group to produce for her because they had respected her intellect and ability, though they hadn't especially liked her. I knew my fellow editors liked me, but I wasn't sure they respected me, and I wasn't sure they'd take orders from me. I wished to heaven I didn't have to find out.

5

I SPENT THE afternoon skimming unsolicited manuscripts, looking for a few that might do for our final issue of the year. I had plenty to choose from, since every young law professor in the country cranks out three or four law review articles a year, hoping to win tenure. The law of averages should guarantee that a few of these will be publishable, but I guess the good articles all ended up at *Harvard Law Review*. They certainly didn't make it to my desk. This particular afternoon, I had a stack of articles with opening sentences like, "Nowhere have egregious judicial dichotomizations been more squarely behind the eight ball than in the conceptualizations of warrantless arrest scenarios in appellate review models."

The articles by practicing lawyers were even worse.

Lawyers adore redundant word pairs (cease and desist, due and payable, will and testament), and they don't know how to use law books (that's what law clerks are for), so editing their articles means completely rewriting them. And staying up till four in the morning reworking an article titled "Rule 10 (b) (5) and Its Application to Debenture and Preferred Share Tender Offers in Closely Held Corporations" can be an existential nightmare, believe me.

Bearing this in mind, I sat in the relative quiet of the inner office, at one of the six desks reserved for "senior staff," stuffing rejection letters into envelopes.

I soon became aware of a presence behind me. Specifically, I felt that a conversation had begun with a silence. I turned to find a lanky young man hesitating at the door of the inner office.

Pause. "I was told I could find the editor-in-chief here?" He was not a law student; I could see that. He was dressed wrong, in rumpled twill slacks, a threadbare corduroy sport jacket, his tie askew. Work clothes belonging to some less formal profession.

"A reporter?" I guessed.

His apologetic features—long nose, wide mouth, close-set brown eyes—registered surprise. He rubbed his right palm along his thigh, then extended it. "Manuel Boyd. *San Francisco Express.*"

A good tabloid, which you could pick up free in art theater lobbies and food co-ops.

I shook his hand. "Willa Jansson."

Pause. "I'm researching a piece on, uh, Susan Green?" He spoke the name as if afraid I'd never heard of her.

"Sit down." I indicated the empty chairs. Not many editors worked in the inner office anymore.

He saw awkwardly, like a stork bending its legs the wrong way. Pause. "Can you just kind of tell me about her, what she was like, what her life was like?"

"She was incredibly smart, very conventional. She was a good writer." I tossed him the latest issue of the review. "She's got an article in this one."

He gave me a look of sweet, gentle curiosity. "Do you have any suspicions about who killed her?"

I was amused. "Of course not."

Pause. "Could you show me where she was sitting? And what exactly she was doing?"

I wheeled my chair-on-casters to Susan's desk. "She was reading an unsolicited manuscript."

"Who by?"

I frowned at the surface of Susan's desk, rubbed dull with cleanser. What the hell had it been? It had gotten soaked with blood and the police had taken it away with them. I stood and walked to the filing cabinet. I pulled a file from the top drawer. It should contain a cover letter for every article that had come in that week. We separated the letters from the articles to be sure we didn't lose return addresses as we passed the manuscripts around.

The manuscripts themselves were filed away according to topic. We kept this slush pile of unpublished research as a source of ideas for "qualified" students (top ten percent) interested in writing articles for law review. The students couldn't plagiarize, of course, but our rejected manuscripts were rarely published elsewhere, and it seemed a waste of good (or more often bad) research not to let students pillage the footnotes for topic ideas.

The manuscripts that had arrived the week of Susan's

murder would be in the filing cabinet somewhere—all but the one the police had taken.

Intrigued, I set to work matching cover letters to manuscripts. The reporter made no sound. I began to feel like some animal, observed in the wild by a nervous naturalist.

It took me about five minutes to look up all the articles. All of them. They were all there. That was troubling.

"I don't know what she was reading. It didn't have a cover letter, so it must have been hand-delivered."

Manuel Boyd sat forward, watching me expectantly.

I watched him back.

"Do you think whoever delivered the article killed Susan Green?"

I shrugged. "It's dangerous work, editing a law review."

6

THE NEXT MORNING I had more visitors. Every time I returned to the law review office from a class or an errand, I found someone there, acting suspicious. Or maybe it was just symptomatic of my state of mind, which was progressively more paranoid.

My first surprise guest was none other than Jane Day,

brilliant lawyer, would-be attorney general, wife of the richest, most publicized lawyer in the city, if not the state.

Clarence Day had made a name for himself by winning two million dollars—a fortune, in 1959—for the estranged family of a wino crushed by a faulty piece of city scaffolding. A young, handsome man with pained blue eyes and a sensitive tic at the corner of his mouth (my trial practice professor urged us to cultivate sensitive tics), Day had actually made the jury weep over the worth of Everyman, be he ever so derelict. Since then, Day had won over a billion dollars in personal injury and class action awards. His contingent fee was never less than one-third of the judgment, so even deducting expenses, the man had to be rolling in green stuff. He owned a castle in Pacific Heights and drove a baby-blue Rolls that set off his eyes to perfection. I'd seen him around town, and I admit, even at sixty, with silver-gray hair and a slackening jawline, there was something dashing about him, a suggestion of the Scarlet Pimpernel aging gracefully.

Jane Day had started out as an associate in Clarence's law firm, an honor accorded only the very eloquent. She'd won a few of his "impossible" cases, and Day had rewarded her by making her his law partner after only three years. She was a small, straight-browed woman, with a retroussé nose and a delicate mouth that hovered between a faint smile and an expression of mild distaste. She dressed with understated elegance, favoring cashmere suits and silk blouses with lace yokes, and she spoke so softly that juries had to strain to hear her—a clever way to make opposing counsel seem boorishly aggressive. Years ago, a local columnist had taken to calling her Lady Jane, and the sobriquet had stuck. When she and Clarence married the year after she made partner, it was San Francisco's royal wedding. Commoners lined the streets to watch ten white Rolls Royces take the wedding party to Grace Cathedral.

No one was surprised when Lady Jane announced her candidacy for attorney general. In the decade since they'd married, she and Clarence had become acknowledged kingmakers. Jane Day had the money and the charisma to make it.

I found her in the law review office quietly flicking through the filing cabinet. I remembered she'd been on campus the day Susan died, and had the kind of moment that made Rod Serling's career.

"Ms. Day?"

She turned, running her fingers over the files. "A trip down memory lane." Nostalgia whispered in her voice. "Did you know I was on law review once?" A smile crinkled the translucent skin around her eyes. "I thought you might still have my student article, but I suppose you don't keep them that long."

To become a law review editor, it isn't enough to "grade on" (be in the top ten percent). A student also has to "write on," submitting an article and having it accepted for publication. If Jane Day had been an editor, then her piece had been published.

I glanced at the bookshelf next to the filing cabinet. It held the back numbers of the review, all eighty-eight years' worth. I would have thought it more natural if Jane Day had sought out the published version of her article. But all I said was, "No, we keep rejected manuscripts a year or two, but we throw out the others as soon as they're in print."

"This enclosed area is new," she observed.

I nodded. "Just this year."

"Well, I won't keep you. I have an appointment with your dean. He should be in by now."

Again I nodded. When she walked past, I could smell Oscar de la Renta, as light as crushed petals.

I waited a moment, then crossed to the cabinet and pulled out the files she'd been fingering. They were edited drafts of Susan Green's article, the one that had just rolled off the presses. In the normal course of events, the manuscripts would have been thrown out the day the issue had been distributed. But that had been the day of Susan's murder, and nothing had taken its normal course.

I took the sheaf of papers to my desk and sat down. There were two drafts, basically the same, though reflecting different stages of editing. The first had been checked for substance. I recognized Mary West's scrawls in the margin. There were few of them. Susan didn't make mistakes in case interpretation, and even if she had, Mary was too indolent to find them. The draft had been heavily edited stylistically, however. Mary hated adjectives and loved action verbs, so that her prose—and every manuscript she edited—read like the sports page.

A second version, retaining few of Mary's changes, showed the meticulous red pencil of John Henderson's technical edit. Margins were filled with instructions to the printer.

The article itself was about campaign financing laws, particularly the disclosure requirements for candidates. It focused on whether, and to what extent, a candidate's family members should be forced to disclose their financial dealings—a subject definitely germane to would-be Attorney General Day. But as far as I knew, Susan had broken no new ground; everything in her article was public knowledge, accessible to Lady Jane and doubtless well understood by her aides.

Still, something in Susan's published article had made Jane Day want to see the earlier drafts.

7

My SECOND SUSPICIOUS visitor of the day was Professor Miles.

I'd refiled Susan Green's drafts and then gone out to scour the upstairs corridors for Tchielowicz. Maddening though he might be, he was amusing, and I needed a light moment. But he was nowhere to be found, and I was nearly crushed to death by a herd of students escaping from a torts class. I decided, with nettled disdain, that Tchielowicz was probably still at the YMCA, paying good money to sweat.

I ran back down the stairs and almost fell over Harold Scharr, who was waiting for me on the bottom step.

"Danger, danger," he warned, rising smooth as a cobra. He was dressed for work (he clerked for the U.S.

attorney four afternoons a week). He wore a one-button, double-breasted suit—perfect on his long, spare frame. "Ginny Miles is ransacking your office."

Two mornings a week, Harold had the misfortune of being Professor Miles' research assistant.

"Why the sudden interest in the damned law review office?"

"Ah, why indeed?" He gave his shirtsleeves a delicate tug, fingering the small platinum cufflinks he affected.

"What's she doing in the office? And how do you know, anyway?"

"I know because I followed her and peeked in. I followed her because I thought that was where she was going. And—to forestall you—I thought so because she's been interrogating me about the law review all morning." He seated me on a white linen handkerchief he'd spread on the grimy stair (I am not usually so fastidious about my bedenimed posterior). Then he pulled a file from his briefcase and sat on that.

"What did she want to know?" I dragged my fingers through my bangs in exasperation.

My dishevelment seemed to pain Harold; he smoothed my hair with the tip of a manicured finger. "Procedural stuff—is there usually someone in the office to take phone calls; who does the final edits; what do we do with manuscripts that are ready to go to the printer's—that kind of stuff. Says she's curious whether things have changed since she was the review's faculty advisor."

"Oh God, she wasn't!"

"Fifteen years ago. See, and you thought things couldn't be worse. She also wanted to know what happened to the stuff in Susan Green's desk. Yes, well may you gape. You know, she practically spits when your name is mentioned.''

''Christ. Are you sure she's still in there?''

''She hasn't come back this way.''

There was one other way out of the basement, through a self-locking door to the faculty garage. Anyone could leave that way, but no one could enter without a key. And there was no other office to duck into down there, just some locked storage rooms.

I stood up. ''Wish me luck.''

''Are you hoping to catch her or miss her?''

''Catch her, of course.''

''That a girl.'' Rising, he gave me a brief hug; I wouldn't have minded more.

I entered the office as quietly as I could and looked around. The outer office had been cut into an L-shape by the plywood-and-acrylic enclosure. The leg of the L was taken up with secondhand couches and chairs, enough to seat most of us during staff meetings. That part of the office was separated from the editors' workroom by sheets of plywood. From there, the inner office was visible only through a window-sized spot where the plywood had run out.

I crept over and peeked through this acrylic window.

Professor Miles was in there, just as I'd known she would be. Unlike Jane Day, she seemed uninterested in the filing cabinets—she was searching the desks. She ignored manuscripts and concentrated instead on notes and slips of paper. There were two rows of three desks each, and I watched her read every little memo in three of them. I assume she'd already done the others (Susan's was empty, thanks to the police), because she turned to leave.

This was my moment, and I wasn't exactly pleased to seize it. But I met her at the door, saying, "Can I help you find something, professor?"

Her bony arms flung up reflexively and her neck jerked. Great, I thought, I've given her a heart attack. But she made a quick recovery.

"No, you cannot, Ms. Jansson." Most professors keep up the Mr. and Ms. stuff outside the classroom, to hold us at arm's length, I suppose. "I am looking for Mr. Scharr, whom you may know is my research assistant."

"I was just talking to him on the stair."

A trace of a frown, hastily stifled. "Then perhaps I can catch him."

She stalked out, leading with the hipbone.

I crossed to my desk and looked through the drawers. Professor Miles had doubtless guessed that I'd recently quit smoking—only an ex-addict would squirrel away so much gum and hard candy. And she'd learned that I clip out right-wing editorials to which I begin, but never finish, scathing responses; that I let bus transfers pile up; and that I'm hopelessly behind in my filing. But whatever she was looking for, she certainly didn't find it in my desk.

8

I THOUGHT I was taking Susan Green's murder very well, considering I worked in the same office and was constantly reminded of her. I was able to go about my business— once Susan's business—because I am not a cerebral person, not at all a ponderer or a brooder. My parents analyze everything to death; they can't eat a piece of toast without discussing the denatured quality of the flour, the immoral investments of the conglomerate that owns the bread company, and the fact that people in Africa are starving.

I'd been to three separate memorial services for Susan, and that was depressing enough. The one at the law school had featured stentorian professors extolling her intelligence, students making insincere speeches about her congeniality, and her parents and other relatives shedding brave tears in a row of seats behind the podium. Dean Sorenson had asked me to stand at one end of that row (John Henderson stood at the other), and I'd spent forty painful minutes imitating an Easter Island statue.

I had no idea why Susan was killed, and I just plain didn't want to think about it.

Unfortunately, it was difficult not to, with people creeping around the office searching cabinets and desks. I was beginning to wonder if Susan had known something it had been unhealthy to know. Sitting at my desk with her manuscripts in front of me, I decided I had better try, in the interest of self-preservation, to figure out what was going on.

It was in this grumpy frame of mind that I had my run-in with John Hancock Henderson.

He materialized at his desk, humphing indignantly. He carried an empty box, which he proceded to fill with his books and memorabilia. I waited until he'd packed away the brass scales of justice and judge's gavel he pretentiously displayed on his desk.

"Do you have to be such a baby, John? How's anything changed since last week? Why can't you just keep doing what you were doing before?"

He sucked in air through white, flared nostrils and turned his back on me. "Your actions have been reprehensible! A calculated insult to me!"

"A calculated insult! Why you blubbering ass! If you think I have to look for backhanded ways to insult you when there's so much I'd love to say to your face—" I stood too quickly, and sent my chair sailing back to ricochet off the wall.

"Children! Children!" Tchielowicz chose that moment to return, his rough-featured face suffused with a post-exercise glow.

I went over and grabbed as much of his arm as my hand would fit around. "Come on!"

Tchielowicz batted his fair lashes at me. "I prefer my dates to phone ahead of time."

I tugged him out the door. "Maybe that's why you never have any."

As we crossed into the corridor, John Henderson bellowed: "I'm going to tell everybody in this school how you cheated me!"

9

"Larry—" I began.

He drew back to look at me in disbelief. "Larry?"

"That *is* your name, isn't it?"

"I didn't think you knew that."

"Look, Tchielowicz, I don't want to spar. I've had a rough morning." I savaged my bangs again and saw a gleam of amusement in his eyes. Unlike Harold, he resisted any impulse he may have had to right them.

He leaned against a storage room door. The corridor smelled of damp mothballs. "Sounded to me like you were holding your own."

"I don't mean that maternity ward for houseflies! Although I'd like to ring Henderson's oily neck! Who am I supposed to get to replace him? Especially with exams coming up."

"What did you say to set him off?"

"Me! I didn't say anything!" I rubbed my arms; it was always cold in that dim corridor. "Anyway, I don't care about Henderson. Screw him."

"After you."

"Larry, look—" I could hear Henderson stomping around the law review office, could hear cars revving in the basement garage. "I'm beginning to think Susan found out something—"

Mary West came tripping down the staircase. I saw the Italian boots first, then the leather mini, then the camisole (certainly a brave display on a typically damp November morning). I shut up; Mary would spread the tale like grass-fire. I looked at Tchielowicz with regret and saw in his expression an intensity I couldn't fathom. It might have been dread, anticipation, sadness, even indigestion. It was gone in a split-second, but I saw it.

When she hit level ground, Mary sang out, "Guess who I've been fucking?"

Tchielowicz's face twitched with disapproval; he'd never appreciated Mary's frank demonstrations of sexual appetite. I guess I'm a little hidebound myself, which is the least of my sexual problems.

"Jake, the beautiful marble god, Whittsen," she trilled, when we failed to respond. Her black hair fanned out behind her as she executed a pirouette.

I'd flirted with Jake, too, fantasized about him, if the truth be known. I'd even flattered myself that we'd have become lovers but for his being an honorably married man. Now I knew better, and it hurt.

I looked at the floor. There was a flattened cigarette butt at my feet. I'd have given anything to smoke it.

Mary, in a postcoital glow, began describing their morning together, and at that I chafed. "Later, Mary." I avoided her eye. "I've got to go."

I walked away quickly, glancing back at Tchielowicz, who watched me through narrowed eyes. I had just announced my wounded pride to him, and that was galling.

I went upstairs to the cafeteria. It was getting on ten-thirty, and the brunch crowd clattered forks and filled the room with shrieks of conversation. Along one wall, a row of pinball machines clanged and rattled as their rugby-shirted operators thumped the metal sides, eyeballed women, and guffawed. It never failed to annoy me that many of these belching, overgrown adolescents understood federal income taxation better than I did.

I bought two cups of coffee, both for me, and sat at a corner table with a friend of mine.

Mario Gilas and I had been to a lot of rallies and marches together over the years. "Willita, we go to the dean today to lobby for a public interest law program. You want to come?"

"No. I'm sick of law. I'm sick of law-related activities."

"So drop off law review. It's a bunch of elitist bullshit, anyway."

There was no arguing with that. But even the left-wing law firm I wanted to work for demanded top ten percent and law review.

"Besides, Willita, I hear you're having problems downstairs."

I guzzled one cup of tepid coffee and felt steady enough to inquire, "Other than the occasional homicide?"

"I hear John Henderson's quitting and that he's complaining about you to some faculty committee today.'' He reached a plump hand across the table and batted down a spike of my hair.

''Faculty committee?'' It wasn't like them to dabble in the affairs of lesser mortals. ''Where did you hear that?''

''Blowing in the wind. I also hear Professor Haas called the meeting for Henderson.''

That straightened my spine. Gunnar Haas, the diffident comparative law professor, was best known for having helped revamp Sweden's criminal code. Since then he'd taught at major law schools in Sweden, Italy, and France. (Apparently that wasn't accomplishment enough, however; I'd overheard a torts professor drawl to Dean Sorenson, ''Haas hasn't published anything this year.'') Though Gunnar Haas had been on Malhousie's faculty for three years, the dean had yet to appoint him to any ''important'' committees; instead he'd made him faculty advisor to the law review. As such, the professor persuaded colleagues at other schools to contribute to our symposia, he helped students polish their articles, and he even got us invited to a few faculty functions.

On top of that, he had classic Swedish features, a darling habit of squinting when he looked up from his lecture notes, and an unexpected sense of humor. He was my major crush number three, right after Jake Whittsen and Harold Scharr.

''I thought Professor Haas liked me. Where did you hear this?''

''I heard Henderson bragging about it. He said Haas was going to get the committee to censure your editorial board.''

I crushed my empty styrofoam cup. "Censure? For not electing Henderson editor-in-chief?"

"Henderson says, for not following the proper chain of succession."

"God." I dropped my forehead to the table. What the hell was going on? Why would Gunnar Haas involve the faculty in a petty student dispute? It made no sense.

But then, Jane Day's behavior, Professor Miles' behavior, Henderson's behavior, even goddam Jake Whittsen's behavior, none of it made sense. What the hell had gotten into everyone?

"You all right?"

I sat up, dodging a shoulder bag as it swung out behind a rushing woman. "If Henderson's got Professor Haas in his pocket, why's he cleaning out his desk? Why doesn't he ask the committee to set aside our vote?"

"Do you think they'd do that?"

I had to shout over the exuberant whooping of the pinball morons. "They hate his smelly innards as much as we do."

Mario shook his head. "I thought Professor Haas was supposed to be an okay guy."

"I thought so, too."

10

ELEVEN O'CLOCK CLASSES had begun, and the office showed signs of hasty abandonment. There were half-full mugs and wet teaspoons on the table, unfolded newspapers on the couches. A schedule of law firms conducting on-campus interviews had been taped to the wall and graffitoed over with rude observations. (The pithiest of these read "Interviewer's underwear too tight.")

I felt a stab of paranoia as I approached the inner office. I'd already had three unpleasant encounters there that morning. Unfortunately, I was about to have a fourth. Standing alone in the office, frowning at Henderson's desk as he pulled open the emptied drawers, was Professor Haas.

"If you're looking for John Henderson—"

The professor stepped sheepishly away from the desk. "No, I think John is rather large for such a drawer."

"Then what are you looking for?" The question I'd longed to ask my two other intruders.

Gunnar Haas' smile was self-deprecating, which had the charm of the unusual in an environment where most took themselves very seriously. "You will be very displeased with me, I fear."

"I'm displeased with everyone this morning. Don't let it worry you."

"But of course it worries me." He stopped looking me in the eye. "I have been speaking with John about who will replace Susan Green. He has asked that I place the matter before the academic credits committee, and I feel that as the law review's advisor I must allow him to air his grievance. But I hope you will not take it too seriously, as it will alter nothing."

A lawyer can put a good face on anything. "It'll cause a lot of talk and legitimize John's tantrums."

He didn't respond. He passed what looked like a pianist's hand over his thin blond hair.

"Why were you going through John's desk?" I wanted one straight answer out of someone, that morning.

"You may imagine the worse, without contradiction." On which cryptic note, Gunnar Haas exited.

11

BY AFTERNOON, HALF the law school would know what Henderson was up to. And what would they do about it? They'd come down to the office to talk to me. I'd have the same conversation forty times, get no work done, and grow more irritated by the hour. I began rifling my desk drawer for cigarettes, then remembered that my parents had finally badgered me into quitting (R.J. Reynolds Tobacco Company engages in immoral investment practices).

I collected my things and slipped out through the faculty garage. I felt like kicking Gunnar Haas' Alfa Romeo, parked near the door. I'd gladly have done the same to Professor Miles' Audi and the dean's Mercedes 450SL. My mother would have been proud; she likes me to show a spark of terrorism.

Malhousie is close enough to San Francisco's Civic Center to be on several bus routes. I grabbed the first bus I saw and rode uptown. On impulse, I got out at the stop nearest Larry Tchielowicz's apartment. I'd been there once or twice with a study group; Tchielowicz had known more about conveyancing than the rest of us combined, but we'd had to pound labor law into his head with a mallet.

I climbed four flights of stairs and rang Tchielowicz's bell.

His roommate, Martin Relke, opened the door, and I pushed past him, looking around the living room for Larry. Martin looked startled, to say the least. His hair was damp, he still carried a towel in one hand, and he was barefoot and shirtless. He had a blank Aryan face and a long, bony torso that reminded me of a giant chicken neck. He was supposed to be very good looking, but maybe you had to be a Republican to see it.

Martin and his preppy friends specialized in drinking beer, playing squash, and bragging that they never dated women law students. Instead, they ordered up busloads of coeds from Mills College for all their parties. They also belonged to something called the Republican Law Students League, whose members all dressed like George Bush.

There's a lot wrong with Tchielowicz, but I thought he might have done better than Right-wing Relke for a roommate.

"Where's Larry?"

Martin shrugged. "Dunno. School, probably. You can join the crowd and wait here for him if you want. I've got a secured transactions class to go to."

The "crowd" came out of the kitchen at that moment, carrying a glass of milk (yes, milk!). She was a smallish, cutish, wholesome-looking girl, a year or two younger than Tchielowicz, dressed in kneesocks, loafers, a plaid skirt, and a blue cardigan.

"Hi. I'm Judy," she informed me, in a chirpy, smiling voice.

I hadn't known Larry's taste ran to chipmunks. "Bye. I'm Willa," I returned, in my usual crabby tones.

I made tracks back to the bus stop.

Ten minutes later, Martin Relke joined me, his jacket slung over his shoulder in macho disregard of the freezing fog. He looked about as convivial as I felt.

"I heard John Henderson's being a jerk," he muttered, craning his neck to watch for the bus.

"You're too easy on him."

Martin shook his head. "How does a turkey like Henderson get a job with Clarence Day's firm?"

"Say that again."

"He was bragging about it at a League meeting last week."

I was still pondering this when the bus pulled up.

12

MALHOUSIE LAW SCHOOL is a few blocks away from San Francisco's Greyhound Bus depot. That's the kind of neighborhood it's in. It's your basic black box of a build-

ing, surrounded by flophouses and porno palaces, which
you can admire from an alabaster patio near the lobby.
There's a short wall along two sides of the patio; you can
chase pigeons off it and sit on their scat if you care to. Or
you can sit on the wide, shallow patio stairs and chat with
the derelicts and bag ladies who lounge there (my mother
does this whenever she visits me at school). Most students
prefer to remain inside and swelter on the top two floors
(the library, faculty, and administrative offices), or freeze
on the bottom two floors (classrooms and cafeteria). Never
in my two and a half years at Malhousie have I seen gath-
erings of students on the patio; I've seen knife fights, raving drunks, teenagers shooting up, even the occasional
student lying in the sun (invariably some naive first-year
from the Sacramento Valley, where they have malls instead
of slums). Most students walk to City Hall or International
Plaza if they want to sit outside. A hint of sunshine and
your nose tells you the most popular use for Malhousie's
patio: the neighborhood is notoriously deficient in public
toilets.

That's why Martin Relke and I stopped and stared when
we saw the crowd spilling off the patio onto the steps.
People pushed past us heading for the school; Channel 7
and Channel 4 news vans were double-parked at a side
entrance. This was baffling enough. Then I spotted Larry
Tchielowicz pacing the sidewalk, watching for something.

It turned out that the something was me. He flailed his
arm in a ''back off'' gesture, and Martin and I stopped
and waited while he trotted over to us.

''Come on,'' he ordered roughly, grabbing my elbow.
He pulled me against the flow of foot traffic, back toward
Market Street. ''Get lost, Relke,'' he added.

"What are all those people doing there?" I had a bad feeling about it. Something had dimmed the sparkle I was used to seeing in Larry's eyes.

"Later. Come on, let's get out of here before someone spots you."

I had a *very* bad feeling about that.

We ended up at a Chinese greasy spoon, the kind with a gloomy interior and bits of winged protein in the stir-fry.

Larry said, "It's Henderson—"

I almost screamed at the sound of his name. Didn't anyone talk about anything else anymore? "What's he gone and done now, called a goddam press conference?"

Larry slid a stubby-fingered hand across the red Formica. "He's gone and got himself killed, Willa. At your desk."

I slumped back against the torn Naugahyde of the booth, and Tchielowicz sidled over and put his arm around me. I could feel the warmth of his body through the cotton knit of his polo shirt, I could smell the no-nonsense soap he'd used at the Y. His hand tightened on my shoulder.

"How did it, was it like—"

"Just like Susan. They don't know what hit him."

A yawning Chinese lady appeared at our table with two water glasses I wouldn't have offered a diseased rat. Tchielowicz refused menus and said we just wanted tea. She snorted and trudged away.

"When did it happen?"

"I don't know. Listen, Willa, did you go back to the office this morning? After we saw Mary?"

I nodded. "I only left about an hour ago. Around eleven-thirty. Right after Professor Haas."

I told him about my run-in with Gunnar Haas. I also told him there was a teenager named Judy waiting for him at his apartment.

"At my—? What were you doing *there*?"

"Making sure Judy didn't spill milk on her pom poms."

"She came by the office this morning." He frowned. "I sent her to my place to wait for me."

I scooted away from him and began making wet rings on the Formica table with my water glass. "What do you mean, Henderson was at my desk?"

"It looked to me like he'd been going through it."

"Looked to you! You *saw* him?"

His jaw clamped tight, and his thick brows furrowed. His hand shook as he lowered his arm from the back of the booth. "Yup. I found him. He was slumped over your desk with a couple of the drawers open and his hand in one of them. It's a hell of a mess, your desk."

For a while neither of us spoke.

I broke the silence. "How'd you get away so fast? How come the cops let you leave?"

The sparkle was back in his eyes. "They don't know I found him. I was out of there in about five seconds. As soon as I made sure he was—"

"Yeah." I pondered this. "So why's the place crawling with police?"

"The police pulled up as I was going outside. Looks like whoever did it called them. Or someone found him before I did."

We brooded over lukewarm tea for another ten minutes. I forgot to tell him about Jane Day and Professor Miles. I was thinking about what was in store for me.

A second and similar murder, the murder of someone who'd announced to all he encountered that I'd cheated him of his rightful editorial position, which I occupied only because someone else had been murdered: the police were bound to wonder (and bound to ask me, for many hours) whether I was a homicidal masthead climber. Even more damning, John Hancock Henderson had been rifling through my desk. What in god's name had he been looking for?

Jane Day, Professor Miles, Gunnar Haas, John Henderson. What in the world had they been looking for?

13

HE WAS A stocky five-foot nine, with a Dudley Do-Right jaw, one black eyebrow transversing the bridge of a broken Italian nose, and the lecherous, self-assured expression of a confirmed jock. He was doing a very bad imitation of bedroom eyes; he was looking at me and seeing a cute little blonde.

"Cops are good guys," he assured me. "We're here to protect you." He smiled, not at me, but at the cute little blonde that I wasn't.

We were in a placement office interview room. In rooms on either side of us, students sweated in broadcloth and worsted, explaining how one capricious contracts or corporations professor had sabotaged a brilliant grade point average.

"Too bad you weren't here to protect John Henderson."

Lieutenant Don Surgelato perched himself on the table top, looking down at me in my folding chair. He was too big for his suit; when he sat, the seams strained nearly to breaking. But then, he looked like he might enjoy exposing a little thigh.

"What was John Henderson looking for in your desk? Drugs?"

"John didn't do drugs."

"But you do?"

"Christ."

"Correct me if I'm wrong; a little pot, but no cocaine or acid—not lately. Right?"

"I don't know what John Henderson was looking for."

"Money or valuables in your desk?"

"No."

"Tell me again where you were this morning."

I told him again.

"Cold morning. Funny you'd leave your jacket behind." He pulled my jacket off one of the three extra chairs in the room. "This is yours, right?"

"Yes."

I reached for it, but he withdrew it. "Sorry, lab has dibs."

"It was over the back of my chair, at my desk." It probably had blood on it; I couldn't think why else the police lab would want it. My favorite jacket, too, a salt and pepper tweed I'd bought in Boston. "I was sick of the office. I wasn't thinking about the weather; I wasn't planning to go far. I just sort of ended up on the bus. On impulse."

"Impulse, huh?" He shook his head. "I hear you didn't get along too well with John Henderson."

I closed my eyes and saw a holy vision: an extra long cigarette with a brown filter and a glowing tip. I could almost smell the smoke, almost smell the nicotine residue on my fingertips.

Surgelato patted my arm, recalling me to reality.

"I hear John Henderson was supposed to be editor of your law review, but you beat him out of it."

"He wasn't 'supposed to be' editor-in-chief. We don't even need an editor-in-chief; we only have one more issue to put out this year. It's just that John— Shit. John thought we did. He went and whined—talked—to the dean about it."

"Okay, I know the type. So the dean—that would be Byron Sorenson?"

"Yes."

"What did Sorenson say?"

"He told us to elect a new editor-in-chief."

"And you won the election? Why you?"

"I'm senior articles editor." Surgelato's cologne was overwhelming in the windowless cubicle.

"Meaning what?"

"Meaning I oversee the editing of all the articles and do most of the final edits myself."

"What did John Henderson do?"

"Checked citations and footnotes. If they don't conform exactly to an established format, a bunch of scholars come out of the woodwork and natter about it. John also proof-read, chose typeface, all the technical stuff.''

''And editor-in-chief?''

''Susan decided which articles we'd publish. She dealt with authors, assigned work, set deadlines, coordinated everything.'' Jesus Christ, I'd have to do all that now. With exams two weeks away.

''Sounds like a headache to me.''

I nodded.

''So why did Henderson want it?''

I could hear a student shuffle into the room next door. ''It looks good on your résumé.''

''How good?''

I shrugged.

''Good enough to make the difference between a hot-shot job in a big firm and a so-so job?''

''Yes.''

''So you wanted it, too.''

I shook my head. ''I've got a job waiting.''

''Good pay?''

''Not especially.''

''What's good pay for a lawyer these days?''

''Forty thousand? I'm not really sure.''

''How much are you going to make?''

''Twenty-two.''

He jerked his thumb at the wall. ''Students next door, they're interviewing, right? Not too late for you to get a better-paying job, is it?''

''Not if I wanted one. But I don't.''

He folded his big arms across his chest and frowned, his eyes lost in the shadow of a neanderthal brow bone. ''Now why is that, Miss Jansson?''

"I'll be working for Julian Warneke."

"Warneke, huh? So it's politics with you." He seemed to waver on the brink of further comment. "What about Henderson? What kind of job was he after?"

"I heard he was going to work for Clarence Day."

"Ambulance chaser? Can't do much better than Day & Day, I guess." He raised one brow. "Doesn't sound like Henderson needed this editor thing on his résumé. Maybe his grudge against you was personal; what do you think?"

"I don't know what to think." I could feel tears welling up. "I only knew him through law review! And it's not like I *wanted* the editors to elect me! I wish— If I'd known—"

He waited for me to continue. When I didn't, he asked me softly, "Anything funny going on at your law review?"

"Oh we're a hilarious group. Especially lately."

"Henderson told everyone he was next in line for editor-in-chief, am I right?"

"Yes."

"So . . . Any reason somebody'd want to kill off your editor-in-chief? I mean, not a particular person, but the editor-in-chief, whoever it happened to be?"

"Jesus! There's a comforting thought."

14

FOR THE WEEK following Henderson's murder, the law review office was locked. Every scrap of paper, every file in the place was dumped out and kicked around the floor by homicide inspectors (or so it appeared).

I let everything slide. I didn't read manuscripts, I didn't assign work, I didn't contact authors.

The police might have let me into the office to do those things, but I didn't ask. For one thing, a flock of reporters shivered on the patio, filming the law school's black facade and interviewing anyone with a yen to be on camera. I must have seen Malhousie's janitor on four different news programs, most of them opening, "It's a somber Thanksgiving for the students of Malhousie Law School. . . ."

I stayed away from Malhousie as much as I could. And when I did try to go to class, Dean Sorenson ambushed me in the corridor and dragged me up to his lair. The dean's fourth-floor office, as big as both rooms of the law review, was ringed with plaster busts of famous jurists. They gave the place a house-of-wax atmosphere; I half expected to find a counter full of souvenir gavels and peri-wig salt shakers.

For over an hour, I listened to the dean wax philosoph-ical about the public's First Amendment right to know. He droned on and on as though he'd found in me the perfect audience; considering our relationship, I was certainly a captive one. I sank into a leather wing chair and suc-cumbed to claustrophobic panic; it was like watching a Trotskyite take the floor of a political meeting.

I decided I'd better hide out for a while, in spite of its being the last week of fall semester classes. Reporters kept phoning me at home, so I went to my parents' house (they were flitting around El Salvador with three nuns from the Resource Center for Non-Violent Studies). I spent the week smoking pot, reading federal income tax regula-tions, and eating Wheatena because it was the only thing in my parents' kitchen.

When I went back five days later, the school was in less of an uproar. Reporters had abandoned the patio to the native pigeon population, leaving behind a blanket of sod-den, scat-spotted litter. Wrapped in damp newspaper in the middle of it was an old man whose glassy-eyed, gray-stubbled face was a fixture around the neighborhood. I slipped him a buck, and he got creakily to his feet and followed me inside, begging, "Plead my case, lady, plead my case?"

Plead My Case, as students called him, occasionally wandered through Malhousie, seeking a lawyer for his ex-istential indictment of "every darned thing."

But not that day. Two security guards stopped us in the lobby. They were young men in crisp brown paramilitary uniforms, not the beer-bellied retirees who usually snoozed there.

One of the brownshirts demanded my student ID. Surprised, I dug through my book bag searching for my wallet. I heard a thump, looked up, and saw Plead My Case sliding down the wall as the other guard handcuffed him.

"Hey! What are you doing?" I grabbed the brownshirt's arm, but he shook off my hand. His partner stepped between us, pushing me back as his partner called the cops on his radio phone.

I wasn't sure if the cops were coming for me or the old rummy, and I was too angry to care. I started making a lot of noise about the Fourth Amendment, and that got me started on society's heartless treatment of the homeless.

"Tell it to the marines," was the guard's response.

Plead My Case, meantime, was making camellike motions with his lips and mumbling that the Vietnamese were taking over the neighborhood. He suggested that the guards go arrest them, right now, because they were multiplying and costing us "tax dollars."

We'd drawn an audience of between-class students, but no one joined me in defending the old wino's right to wander through the lobby. In fact, my fellow students were looking at him with malevolent distrust. It astonished me that they could fear a toothless, addled old man so much and fear an armed guard so little.

A uniformed cop finally showed up, and I went through my Fourth Amendment spiel again. The cop found me no more intimidating than the guards had. He skipped the repartee, though, and dragged the old vagrant away "for questioning."

So I was already in a foul mood when I went down to the basement office. I found the coffee urn full of cold, sloshy mold after a week of disuse, and my mailbox was full of memos from the dean requesting further meetings and memorializing his every emotional response to Henderson's murder. I was glad I'd stayed away.

Also in my mailbox were personal notes from faculty members expressing perfunctory condolences while urging me to get the summer issue out on time. There were even a few frantic letters from authors wondering if the murderer had stolen their manuscripts (that would certainly have laid the groundwork for an insanity defense).

The inner office looked like a scene from *Poltergeist*. Files had been dumped everywhere, books heaped on the floor, the bookcase littered with paper coffee cups in sticky puddles, flow charts and corkboards torn from their brackets, filing cabinets rummaged and their contents tossed like salad makings.

The dean arrived while I surveyed the chaos.

I let him talk for a while before I began listening. From his tone I gathered he was repeating something I should have heard the first time.

"If you care to relocate—relocate, my dear—Ms. Jansson?"

"Relocate?"

"The faculty has agreed to turn over a portion of the faculty library to you." He stared at my bangs, and I hastily tidied them.

The faculty library was on the fourth floor, near the faculty offices. It was a well-ventilated set of rooms with oak tables, wing chairs, and leather-bound volumes of state and federal appellate cases. It was an oasis of fresh air, in fact. Two second-year students had leaped to their deaths after a moot court competition the year I started law school; rather than reduce the pressure on its students, the administration had chosen to seal off all third- and fourth-floor windows except those in the faculty offices and faculty library.

The dean continued, "It would require some remodeling, of course, but we could have you moved upstairs by the end of Christmas holidays."

"That might be best."

He nodded, then spent several minutes assuring me that the memorial service for John Henderson had gone smoothly. I said I was glad.

I typed out a memo telling the other editors that our office would be moved over vacation and that I would wait until then to parcel out editorial chores. I wished them luck on exams, wished them happy holidays, and went back into hiding at my parents' house.

Six days later, I rode the streetcar to Malhousie, my lucky pencil in my hand and a thousand treasury regulations jumbled in my brain. I felt like the bottom of a cat box as I signed in to take my federal income tax exam. I looked around and saw my fellow students clutching rag dolls, compulsively downing M&Ms, crossing themselves, even wiping away tears. I wondered what the bar exam would do to us.

I limped out of the exam room four hours later and found half a dozen editors lying in wait for me in the hallway. Tchielowicz stood in the background, though I spotted him first. His expression was wooden, and his short, ash-blond hair had thinned on top—a common enough condition during finals week.

In contrast, Mary West seemed about to bubble over; her cheeks were feverishly flushed, and she had one strong finger hooked into Jake Whittsen's belt loop.

Greg Parker was there too, his pants hitched up over an incipient belly, and his wire-frame glasses sliding down his twitching nose. Chubby and chinless, Greg looked like a hairless guinea pig. Out of his hearing, we called him Nosy, because of his character as much as his last name. He seemed to believe that if he could only find out enough about us, he'd be one of us. He snooped tirelessly. He'd even wished me a happy birthday one day when I'd left my mail—including a sealed birthday card—in my desk drawer. Greg had been one of John Henderson's underlings, and I realized as soon as I saw him there, standing with editors who viewed him as the missing link between humans and banana slugs, that he expected to replace Henderson as executive editor. He peered shortsightedly over Hatty McPherson's shoulder as she skimmed her class notes. She recoiled, frowning, when he accidently touched her shoulder.

Like Greg, Hatty McPherson was a technical editor. Unlike Greg, she was considered one of the foxiest students at the school. She had fluffy blond hair, a pale China doll face with round blue eyes, a button nose, and a pouty little rosebud of a mouth. She always wore frilly dresses and the high-heeled, wooden-soled sandals that are sometimes called CFMQs, for "come fuck me quickly." Hatty was a good technical editor, when she wasn't having a nervous breakdown over deadlines. Unfortunately, this was most of the time. She was nervous to the point of hysteria from her constant dieting, and her trembly eruptions had resulted in Mary West's *chef d'oeuvre* of nicknames, "Mad-as-a-Hatty."

Harold Scharr stepped forward, his brilliant eyes and romantic pallor enhanced by a black turtleneck sweater. "Willa! What a coincidence, meeting you here like this."

He took my arm, guiding me down a flight of stairs and past the brownshirts at the main entrance. The rest of the coterie followed. We went to a bar, a beer and popcorn place, and over the first pitcher, Harold did a morbid, but very funny rendition of the dean's eulogy to the departed Henderson. Hatty nearly dissolved into a fit of nervous twitches, but the rest of us drank and laughed, like patrons at a comedy show.

It was hard to ignore the tensions at the table, though. Jake, looking exhausted and unshaven, pulled away slightly whenever Mary touched him. Mary, again half-frozen in the barest of camisoles, stretched till she nearly popped her lace straps, but she couldn't get Jake's attention. She did cause Parker to sweat till he could hardly keep his glasses on his nose, however.

My eye kept wandering back to Tchielowicz, who sipped his beer and memorized the table top. I hadn't seen him for almost two weeks. He really wasn't so bad-looking, I realized. I'd always thought he looked like a troll, with his large face, low brows, bent nose, and small eyes. But he did have a good build, no denying that, and though you'd never call him handsome, his expression was uncommonly intelligent, and his smile quick.

Over the second pitcher, I came back from the dead. "Okay, Harold. Intermission. I appreciate your tact. Now what's up?"

Harold grinned. "Where ya *been*?"

"Utterly crabbed out in the privacy of my parents' flat. They're in El Salvador right now."

Harold whistled. "I hear it's nice there this time of year."

"Well, they're not your typical tourists. Who's been looking for me?"

"Who hasn't?"

"In that case, I'm glad they didn't find me."

"I don't blame you. But Chief, what now?"

"Nothing."

Harold abandoned his lighthearted pose. "Look, if we move upstairs to the faculty library, we'll spend half our time making academic small talk with the professors." He shuddered theatrically. "I'd rather stay in the basement, unless you feel you can't work down there anymore."

I glanced at the other editors, but knew what I'd see. They wouldn't have joined Harold if they didn't agree with him.

I shrugged. "I can live with it. You want me to talk to the dean today?"

"Tomorrow will do. Keep drinking."

So we met in the law review office five days later, on the last day of finals. My head was still throbbing from an environmental law exam that morning and a consumer credit final that afternoon. My right arm ached to the elbow from gripping my lucky pencil too tightly, and it took several shots of tequila to work the cramp out of my fingers.

We sorted files, made stacks of scratch paper out of old manuscripts, and put the books back onto the shelves. I composed a high-handed memo that began, "Since the majority of you have requested that we remain downstairs . . .'' and put a copy in each editor's box, hoping no one would quit as a result. I rewarded Nosy Parker for his housecleaning diligence by making him acting executive editor, and I chose six manuscripts for the summer issue, my sole criterion being whether the authors were likely to obstruct the editing process with displays of pompous indignation (the closer to tenure, the more years in practice, the greater the pomposity factor, we had found). I distributed the manuscripts for a first edit, moved the pins around on the flowchart—the most fun part of the job—and stole some mistletoe from the cafeteria so I could kiss Jake and Harold. Everyone left in a good mood, and Tchielowicz hung back to escort me out.

At least, that's what I thought. It turned out Tchielowicz had something to show me. It was a page of uniformly small, backslanting capital letters, written in green ink. It read, 'To the Remainderman the following . . .' and it described three pieces of real estate.

It startled me out of my cozy tequila fog. Susan Green had frequently affected green ink and she'd never written in cursive. "Where did you find it?"

"In the mountain of papers near the filing cabinet. Must have been tucked away in a drawer with Susan's class notes."

The cop who'd pulled the sheaf of class notes out of the filing cabinet must have recognized Susan's green ink and shown the pages to the officer supervising the search.

"I suppose this page looked like a bunch of conveyancing jargon to that muscle-brained police lieutenant."

"The Surge?" Tchielowicz grinned. "He's a smart guy. Used to be quarterback for—"

"Oh, football players are notoriously clever."

"There must be a hundred pages of Susan's notes in here. It's not surprising the guy didn't see the significance of this one page."

Lieutenant Don Surgelato obviously hadn't realized that a "remainderman" is someone who inherits part of an estate. He hadn't realized the paper might be part of a holographic, or handwritten, will.

Tchielowicz gestured toward several garbage bags full of crumpled paper. "We should probably look for the rest of it."

My inelegant but heartfelt reaction was, "Shit."

"Well, if it is Susan's will, it's probably the only copy; people don't usually take the trouble to handwrite a will more than once."

So we combed through all the damned papers again, looking for more green ink. We skimmed Susan's convey-ancing and commercial paper notes until I saw the red negative of her green ink whenever I closed my eyes. But we didn't find anything else that looked like a holographic will.

Tchielowicz sighed and began stuffing paper back into garbage sacks. "Want to go with me to the recorder's of-fice tomorrow?"

"All right." A title search would at least tell us if the property on the list belonged to Susan; if it didn't, then the paper wasn't a will, and it was no use turning it over to the police. "You're not going home for the holidays?" I realized I didn't know where "home" was for Tchielo-wicz.

He shook his head, turning his face away. I could see a flush creep up his tree trunk of a neck. He mumbled something about the title search. But I was suddenly curious about him.

"Where are you from, Larry? Where's your family?"

"The army's my family," he said lightly.

"I didn't ask who put you through school. I asked where you're from."

He nudged aside a bag full of garbage, then looked me in the eye, almost pugnaciously. "I was in an orphan asylum in Indiana till I was fourteen. Then the state took care of me for a while."

"The state?"

"I was in a 'correctional educational facility for juveniles,' as they called it."

"You? You're joking. What did you do?"

"Put up with it."

"No, I mean what were you there for?"

"Three years."

"No—Larry, you know what I'm asking you."

"Do *you* know what you're asking me?" His tone was bitter, and he looked angry.

I was stung. Luckily, we were interrupted at that moment, or I'd have made some dumb, inappropriate joke; it's a habit of mine, a make-things-worse reflex.

Jake Whittsen pushed through the door. He looked from me to Tchielowicz and back. He hesitated.

"Mary let you out of her sight?" My gaiety sounded forced, even to me. I extended my hand to him. "I'd like to make her regret it."

Jake looked surprised, but he took my hand. In fact, he kissed it. "I thought you might need a lift someplace. You, too, Larry. My car's out front."

Tchielowicz shook his head. "No. Thanks. Merry

Christmas.'' He sidled past us, slamming the door as he left the office.

Jake squinted down at me. ''Sorry if I interrupted something.''

''I'm glad you did! We were talking about Susan—very morbid. Tchielowicz is usually a lot of laughs, but not today. But hell, what can you expect from a guy who joins the fucking army?''

Jake took a step backward, blinking.

''I'll buy you dinner,'' I offered. ''If you're free.'' If anyone is less free than a married man with a loud-mouthed lover, I don't know who it could be.

Smiling, he offered me his arm. I could smell his cologne, just barely.

Jake had a Volkswagen squareback with Alaska plates. It suited him; he looked like a man from rough, lonely country. He was tall and well built, with dark wavy hair and a wide, noble, expressionless kind of face. I sat close to him in the squareback and decided I was in the mood to fall in love.

I'm usually quite adept at falling in love, but that evening, in spite of a candlelit dinner and a good bottle of wine, my heart remained my own.

''What's Melissa doing?'' I inquired over after-dinner liqueur that tasted like throat lozenges. I'd met Jake's wife the spring before at a law review banquet. She'd been wearing a skin-tight, spaghetti-strapped black dress, which she'd definitely had the body for, damn her. She'd told me she was an artist and a museum curator, that she was fluent in French and Italian. I'd written Jake off that night.

''I don't know and I don't care.''

In my experience, such statements can't be taken at face

value. "I know you've been seeing Mary. Are you and Melissa on the outs?"

Unlike Tchielowicz, Jake did not imply that I should mind my own business. He simply said, "She's seeing someone else. As far as I'm concerned, we're through."

He leaned across the small table and touched his lips to mine. Jake has coffee-colored eyes that grow soft and unfocused when he smiles. It would take a dead libido to withstand them. I wasn't in love, but I was damn well going to give myself a chance.

We went to his place. It was artsy, starkly underfurnished, with gargantuan prints on the walls, and bare wood floors.

He took me in his arms.

And I began to worry about The Problem, cursing my luck for the thousandth time. Should I tell him at the outset, or wait till the last minute? The virus wasn't active; maybe I could just skip the surgeon general's warning this time.

The sound of footsteps interrupted my brooding, and Melissa Whittsen entered the room. I pressed closer to Jake because my shirt was unbuttoned. In fact, Melissa— her eyes dramatically shadowed and her black curls artfully tousled—looked so outraged that I buried my face against Jake's chest and closed my eyes. Finally, I heard her run back through the hallway, slam the front door, and clomp down the stairs.

I was shaken, and Jake kept his arms around me, but it was like embracing a cigar store Indian. (My parents hate me to say Indian, but cigar store Native American doesn't sound right.) I suggested that we take a raincheck, and he drove me home looking bleak as an Alaskan winter. I didn't invite him in, but he hardly seemed to notice.

15

TCHIELOWICZ WAS TRUE to his word. He stopped by for me on his way to the recorder's office. When I answered the door, he peered in disdainfully. "You alone?"

"Not by choice," I drawled. "The missus walked in on us." I saw contempt flicker in his eyes and thought, Who the hell are you to disapprove?

An auspicious start to the day.

We climbed into Tchielowicz's ancient pea-green Chevrolet, and I asked, "Army issue?"

"Summer jobs."

"What'd you join the army for, Larry?"

"No one else volunteered to send me to college."

"How are you going to feel about it when your classmates are rolling in dough and you're a dogface?"

"Dogface? Where'd you hear that?" He glanced at me, a smile back in his eyes. "Look, Gandhi said if you expect to enjoy the benefits of a society, you've got to be willing to go to its defense."

"He also said there were many causes for which he'd die, but none for which he'd kill."

"Are you pro-abortion?"

"No, I'm pro-choice."

"Then there's at least one cause for which you'd kill."

We began to argue in earnest—at least, I argued in earnest. I suspect Tchielowicz argued for sport. It seemed no time at all before we'd reached our destination.

I'd never done a title search before, and as far as I knew, neither had Larry. But he seemed to know what he was doing. He led me to a microfiche machine and began flipping through microfiche cards indexed by grantors' and grantees' last names. We looked for Susan's name, but she had neither bought nor sold the parcels listed in her "will." So we tried several other names, names of editors, names of professors, and wasted half an hour looking up their landholdings. Then I remembered Jane Day's interest in Susan's manuscript and, on a whim, looked under her name and her husband's. And that led to the information we were looking for: the three pieces of property on Susan's list had been deeded within the last five years to Clarence Day.

"Clarence fucking Day!" I marveled. "Why would Susan make a list of Clarence Day's property? And why only these three parcels?" The man owned half the Marina and most of Hunter's Point, it seemed.

"What made you look up Clarence Day?"

I told Tchielowicz about Jane Day's visit to the law review office.

"Free association. Good work, Nancy Drew."

He jotted down the names and addresses of the grantors, as they appeared on the grant deeds (the names meant nothing to us), and we went back to the Chevy to go take a look at the three properties.

On the way, I remembered something else Tchielowicz might not know. "John Henderson was going to go to work for Day after the bar exam."

Larry shook his head. "That's not what I heard."

"Your own reactionary roommate told me."

He frowned at Market Street traffic. "Do you know why John wanted the title 'editor-in-chief'?"

"Résumé."

"Sure, résumé. But specifically because he wanted to work for Wailes, Roth." Wailes, Roth, Fotheringham & Beck is one of the most prestigious rat mazes on Wall Street. "Didn't you ever wonder why he flew to New York all the time?"

"I can honestly say I didn't wonder why he did anything."

I noticed the habitual curl of the upper lip on the right side of Larry's mouth. It was cute.

"I could have sworn someone told me Henderson got that Wall Street job. In fact, I think it was Greg Parker. Greg and I were looking at the on-campus interview schedule the morning Henderson got—" He shook his head.

"Maybe Relke was wrong. Let's call Parker later and ask him about it."

We spent the rest of the morning looking at Clarence Day's real estate. All three parcels were south of Market Street, not far from Malhousie, in a district of dilapidated warehouses. Each showed signs of having once been developed, but aside from weedy chunks of concrete and some old pipe, the lots were now vacant. None was particularly large, not large enough to make us suspect a land development scam, and all were bordered by struggling manufacturing plants and car repair places. Their relationship to Susan Green was not apparent.

At Larry's suggestion, we went to the zoo for lunch. The animals looked cold and lethargic under a heavy gray sky. Plastic Christmas garlands flapped in the icy wind, and I sorely missed my tweed jacket from Boston. I shivered in my sweater and was grateful for the hot dog Larry bought me at a concession. I watched him stuff a foot-long into his face, and I inhaled the steam from a styrofoam cup of coffee. I was almost ready to forgive R.J. Reynolds its immoral investments.

"Why'd you go to law school, Larry?"

He aimed a wadded napkin at a clown-shaped garbage receptacle and seemed pleased when it sailed in. "There aren't many interesting careers in the army. Not if you lack an aptitude for math, which I do."

"You going to be a career army, then?"

A sidelong glance. "Look, I guess I owe the army six years, but I'm sure that'll be enough for my taste."

"Six years is a long time."

"Only if you go into it with a bad attitude."

"What exactly will your job be?"

"Defending soldiers who get into trouble, who commit crimes or break military law. Or desert, or go AWOL, or file for conscientious objector status."

I examined his profile, the way his broad brow overpowered his pug nose and small eyes. And I decided that being defense counsel for a bunch of kids in trouble with the army was a damned admirable job.

He turned to me, grinning. "And you'll parlay your top

five percent, editor-in-chief résumé into a lucrative career defending insurance companies.''

''Not me. I have an understanding with Julian War-neke.''

''Warneke, huh? I should have guessed.''

Julian Warneke ran a stolidly, unimpeachably old-left law firm that did a little fundraising, a little lobbying, a lot of *pro bono* proselytizing, and even some dull old law-yering. ''They defend my mother and father all the time. Hiring me is their way of giving my parents a rebate, I think—sort of a frequent protesters' plan.''

We found a pay phone and I called the three people who'd sold Clarence Day the real estate on Susan's list. My line was, ''I'm interested in a piece of property at such and such an address. A friend of mine, Susan Green, said you own it?''

This got no reaction beyond ''Sorry, I sold it'' from the first two people I phoned. But my third call, to a Mrs. Jeanette Koenig, had unexpected results.

Mrs. Koenig was silent for a long moment. Then she whispered, ''Who is this? What do you want?''

I gestured for Larry to join me in the phone booth. ''My name is Willa Jansson. I—''

''Oh. You.''

''Mrs. Koenig, do I know you?''

''We met at the memorial service.''

I wracked my brain. Susan's memorial service? The students, the faculty had been there. I'd talked to some reporters, but Mrs. Koenig sounded like an elderly woman.

''You're Susan's aunt.'' The row of family members behind the podium, a well-powdered aunt had been among them.

"That's right. What are you asking about the warehouse for? Did Susan tell you about the lawsuit?"

"She said a few things about it," I lied. "I don't want to disturb you, but do you think you could find a few minutes to talk to me and my friend? He also knew Susan."

Another silence. "It's still . . . very painful for me." I wondered whether she referred to the lawsuit or to Susan's death. "But I suppose if you think it's important?"

"Oh, yes, it is important, honestly," I assured her, noticing Larry's smile of surprise. I trailed off, realizing it probably wasn't important at all.

Mrs. Koenig gave me a Pacific Heights address and rang off.

16

MRS. KOENIG HAD the top floor of a well-landscaped, two-story stucco house. The iron grillwork at the door and windows proclaimed that the occupants, like all their neighbors, were well-to-do. We rang her bell, and Mrs. Koenig came downstairs, gripping the brass banister with both hands. She peered at us through the filigree.

I introduced Larry, made a few remarks about hating to trouble her, and wished to god she'd quit vacillating and let us in. It was beginning to drizzle.

Her flat was elegantly conventional, with lots of Dresden shepherdesses, marble table tops, and fleecy white carpet. We sat on Victorian satin furniture and ate some stale gingersnaps she'd arranged on a Limoges tray. Beside me on a mother-of-pearl whatnot was a studio portrait of Susan Green; it was creepy having her look over my shoulder.

"Mrs. Koenig, Susan mentioned that you sold your Howard Street lot to Clarence Day."

She regarded Susan's portrait, her blue-powdered eyelids fluttering. "My 'lot?' Did he tear down the plant, then?"

"Yes, he must have. There's nothing there now."

She shook her tidy silver coiffure, and her mouth became a railroad track of wrinkles. "Well that's too bad. The plant was jobs for sixteen people, once. It was more like a storage place by the time Kendall died, but still, that's jobs, too. And Mr. Day, he said he'd leave it. For the jobs, you know! But you can't trust anybody anymore." She watched Tchielowicz suspiciously.

"So the lawsuit you mentioned on the phone—Clarence Day was your attorney?"

"That's why I sold him the plant! All the expenses after we lost the court case! Just the trial, what it cost me—expert witness fees, document fees, investigators, court fees, jury fees! Everything had a price tag. Mr. Day, he put it all on my account and said not to worry because he'd take it out of my share when we won."

Tchielowicz and I exchanged glances.

"Well we didn't win," she sniffed. "And it cost me a pretty penny, too. I had to sell Mr. Day the warehouse, just to pay the court!"

She told us about the lawsuit Clarence Day had lost for her.

When Mr. Kendall Koenig, brother of Susan's mother, began succumbing to lung cancer, he'd asked his accountant—"a very upstanding young man, we thought"—to recommend a lawyer to draw up an estate plan. The accountant recommended someone he'd met at a party. He'd acquainted the lawyer with the Koenig's financial records, and the lawyer had drawn up a will which had included a trust fund for Mrs. Koenig. When Kendall Koenig died a few months later and it was time to probate the will and set in motion the terms of the trust, Mrs. Koenig found that her "lawyer" had given a fictitious address. The trust assets had been plundered, and the will was so poorly drafted as to be declared invalid. Mrs. Koenig inherited her husband's property by the rules of intestate succession but paid quadruple the death duties she'd have paid had the assets been properly sheltered. She'd had to sell their "lovely homes" and was now forced to live in reduced circumstances in her twelve-room apartment.

The "lawyer" had never been found, but Mrs. Koenig had sued her accountant because she "just knew he'd been in on it, even if he said he wasn't." The accountant had been covered by malpractice insurance, so Clarence Day had sued for two million dollars in actual damages and ten million punitive.

"But I'll tell you where that Mr. Day made his mistake: he let them put two coloreds on the jury! Those people hate anyone with money—I told Mr. Day that! They just don't understand you've got to have money to do good in this world!'' Her cheeks drooped and her eyes glazed with tears.

"What became of the accountant?"

"They took away his license. State board said he was negligent, even if the jury didn't think so. He went away somewhere."

"Do you remember his name?"

"I'll never forget it! Walter Bonomini!"

Tchielowicz spoke for the first time. "Did Clarence Day suggest that you sell him your property?"

"You tell me what else I could have done, young man!"

"Did you sell it directly to Day, or did you offer it for sale to the public?"

She flushed under her powder, her skin becoming as pink as bubblegum. "The court had this different way of selling it."

"A judicial sale?"

"Mr. Day bought it the same morning."

"Did he give you a good price for it?"

She sat up straight and frowned at him. "Yes he did, but he could afford it! What's this got to do with my niece, anyhow?"

That seemed to be our cue to leave.

Tchielowicz wiped the moisture from the inside of the Chevy's windshield, saying, "Well, Nancy Drew, what do you think?"

I used to love Nancy Drew, used to love it when her friends gushed, "Gee, Nancy, you're *so* smart!"

"Buying your client's property at a judicial or probate sale is an infraction of the state bar's Canons of Legal Ethics. Susan was going to rat on Clarence Day, and she was making a list of other property he'd bought from his clients.''

Tchielowicz frowned. ''But let's face it, the rule's there to prevent lawyers from making money off their clients' misfortunes. The state bar's not going to discipline a lawyer who pays market value. It sounds to me like Day was trying to help the old lady out.''

No ''you're so smart, Nancy,'' for me.

''What do you think, then?''

Tchielowicz shook his head. ''If Susan went to the trouble of tracing title to every piece of property Day owns, she must have been after something sexier than a technical infraction.''

''Maybe she thought Day had purposely bungled her aunt's case. It should have been a winner—an insured accountant turning trust assets over to an impostor! And Day's supposed to be the best trial lawyer in the state.''

''So Day lost the case on purpose?'' Tchielowicz turned to me, brows raised and lips curling. ''Along with his thirty or forty percent of a multi-million-dollar judgment? Not too likely, Ms. Drew.''

17

OUR NEXT STEP, we decided, was to get hold of Nosy Greg Parker and find out what he knew about John Henderson's job offers. We went to the law school to find Greg's home phone number, on file in the law review office.

Two brownshirts stopped us in the lobby, demanding our student IDs. I didn't have mine on me.

"But I know you recognize me!"

The guard who'd handcuffed Plead My Case smirked at his fellow guard, Adam's apple bobbing. "No ID, no admittance."

They were still laughing when Tchielowicz dragged me outside for a quick conference. I ended up going in through the faculty garage, and Tchielowicz opened the basement door for me.

The office was pitch-black till we clicked on the overhead fluorescent tubes, and for a moment I was almost afraid we'd find another dead body. But all we found was the usual messy basement room, with its unsightly overhead pipes and its cement-and-pegboard walls.

I dug up a list of editors' phone numbers and phoned Greg. His wife, whom I remembered as a homely woman with too many teeth and over-large gums, answered at the first hint of a ring.

"Greg?" Her whisper was anxious.

Uh-oh. "No. This is Willa Jansson, Patricia. I take it Greg's not home?"

"No. Where are you?"

"At the law review office."

"He's not there?" There was panic in her voice.

I was sitting in the reception area of the L-shaped outer office. A few sheets of acrylic and a too-short door separated me from the inner office. I glanced into the enclosure: nobody, alive or dead. But I did notice a manila envelope on my desk; it hadn't been part of the clutter when I'd left the day before.

"No, he isn't. Was he coming here?"

"He said he was. But that was this morning, early. He missed choir practice at ten, and he didn't pick me up at work at noon like he was supposed to."

You'd have to know Greg Parker to appreciate the gravity of this. Technical editors tend to be extreme anal retentives, dedicated to keeping their pocket calendars current. They do not make spontaneous changes in their plans, they do not miss appointments.

"Do you want me to ask the security guards if they saw him today, Patricia?"

"I already did that. The man said he didn't remember seeing Greg."

Greg Parker wasn't exactly Mr. Memorable, though. "The guard might be brushing you off. Or someone might have let Greg in through the faculty garage door. That's how I got in.''

"He should have quit the review, Willa. I told him he should have, with everyone getting murdered.'' She began to cry.

Another voice came on the line. Patricia's sister asked if I could call back later.

"Has Patricia called the police?''

"Oh yes. Hours ago.''

I gave Patricia's sister my home phone number and asked her to call me when she had news.

Tchielowicz had heard enough to figure out what was wrong. "Wait here a minute. I'm going to look around for him.''

I sat at the desk toying with the phone cord for a while, trying to imagine some circumstance that would account for Greg's absence. Any circumstance but murder.

I glanced through the acrylic partition again and saw the manila envelope on my desk. I almost dreaded going in there and finding out what it contained. I didn't want any more surprises.

I was standing at my desk staring down at the plain, sealed envelope when Mary West charged in.

Her square-jawed face was flushed, her hair disheveled, and she looked furious. She wore leather again, tall boots, a flight jacket, tight black jeans. She stalked to my desk and glared at me.

"You fucking turncoat bitch,'' she spat.

Tchielowicz appeared at the door to the inner office, but he didn't come in. He leaned against the doorframe, big arms folded, watching Mary.

To say I was shocked is an understatement. I picked up

the envelope mechanically because I'd been about to do that when Mary burst in. Then I just stood there.

She took another step toward me, and I was glad the desk was between us. "I thought you had a little more class than to go fucking Jake behind my back."

I looked at Larry, I guess for support. But his eyes were hard, and he shook his head as though Mary had confirmed his low opinion of my morals.

"I called Jake's wife this afternoon, and you know what she said to me?"

"You phoned his *wife*?"

"That's right," Mary said defensively. "She's been screwing around on Jake, and I called to tell her she doesn't deserve him."

"Jesus Christ! You phoned the man's *wife*?"

"Why not? I've got a right to tell her what I think of her jerking Jake around. She should realize someone else will take care of him if she doesn't."

"Does Jake know you called her?" I felt sorry for him; my impression was that he still loved Melissa.

"This is between me and her."

"Don't you think he's got a right to fight his own domestic battles?" I dragged my fingers through my hair and longed for a smoke.

"You goddam hypocrite! You know what Melissa said when I called her? She asked me if every woman in the goddam office was screwing Jake; she said she walked in on you two last night!"

She put her hands on my desktop and leaned toward me, face white with rage. I should have told her nothing had happened between me and Jake after all, but my brain went into its sponge mode. All I could do was soak in the tableau: Mary in the foreground, eyes blazing, and Larry behind her in the doorway, face reflecting profound contempt for the both of us.

Later I might find humor in Mary's outrage at my "betrayal" of her with her married boyfriend. But at that moment it didn't seem funny at all. I backed away till I was up against the wall.

We were frozen in time and space that way for what might have been ten seconds, then Mary announced, "I'll make you sorry for this, Willa!" She pushed past Larry, and a few seconds later I heard the tattoo of her Italian heels in the corridor.

I didn't look at Larry; I knew I wouldn't like what I saw on his face. He said, "Well, if you're ready to go, shall we?"

He drove me home without speaking to me. Damn him, we were supposed to be friends; where did he get off being sanctimonious over something he knew nothing about?

When we finally got to my place, I said, in the most frigid of tones, "Would you care to come in?"

And he replied, "No thanks. I'm taking Judy to a show."

18

I WENT STRAIGHT to my pot drawer, tossing the manila envelope onto my chronically unmade bed. I rolled myself a big fat joint and smoked the whole damn thing, right down to the last bit of gummy paper.

I kept staring at the envelope. I moved a little closer, stepping over a pair of boots and a pile of books. I stood there awhile.

Smoking pot makes me stupid. I don't mind that; being stupid makes a lot of things more interesting (federal income tax is not among them). It also exaggerates my dread of the unknown. And I definitely had a superstitious fear of that manila envelope.

My fear was justified, too. It contained an anonymous note. In neat IBM Selectric type (we have three Selectrics in the office, so I should know), it read: "Investigate Larry Tchielowicz. He was incarcerated in Indiana for attacking someone with a baseball bat."

I reread it. I was so stoned that I had to, just to make sense of the words.

Tchielowicz told me he'd been in a correctional facility

for juveniles—but attacking someone with a baseball bat; it was in a different class than shoplifting or joyriding. I imagined what a baseball bat would do to human tissue and wondered what on earth had incited Larry to do that kind of damage. It was a line of thought I didn't want to pursue.

But the note proved one thing: Greg Parker had been to the law review office that morning. Juvenile records are usually sealed by court order when a minor turns eighteen, and Tchielowicz wasn't the type to confide in his classmates (as I well knew). Only the most officious and determined kind of meddler, snooping through desks, reading other people's mail, eavesdropping on private phone calls, could have sniffed out Larry's secret. And of all the people with access to the office Selectrics, only Parker had elevated nosiness to an art form.

I glanced at my telephone (it was on the floor, half buried in underwear). I knew I should call the police and tell them about the note showing Parker had been to the office. It might help them find him.

It might also make trouble for Larry Tchielowicz (I savored the thought for a moment). The cops probably already knew about the baseball bat incident (Jesus, a baseball bat!), but they didn't know Parker shared the knowledge. Parker wasn't malicious; I couldn't see him ratting on Tchielowicz. It was more his style to pass the information anonymously to a friend and let that person deal with it.

Which left me with the option (and nobody hates options more than a pothead) of ratting or not ratting.

Greg Parker discovers Larry Tchielowicz's secret, then disappears. How would that look to a homicide lieutenant?

On the other hand, why should I protect a moralistic ass like Larry Tchielowicz?

I began to cry. Damn Larry! Damn his milk-fed girl-friend, damn Mary West, and damn Jake Whittsen too. I cried until I fell asleep—passed out, actually.

I woke up to a ringing telephone. I groped for the receiver, failed to untangle the cord, and ended up on the floor with it.

"Willa? Gunnar Haas here."

"Oh." I unsnarled a sock from the spiraled cord and scooted away from a killer dustball. "Hello."

"I wonder if you will be in town Christmas Eve, Willa?"

"Yes."

"The dean is having a cocktail party and I hope you will care to go with me. The faculty enjoys socializing with the students, you know, with the bright ones like yourself."

Considering they treated us like rabble in a plague year, I doubted it. "Well, I don't know. I guess so."

"I can pick you up at six o'clock, if that is acceptable?"

"Six is fine."

"Good. I look forward to seeing you, Willa."

I could have kicked myself for agreeing to squander my Christmas Eve on a group of people I'd gladly never see again. But how do you say no to a man who sounds like he just stepped out of an Ingmar Bergman movie?

19

I WAS STILL getting phone calls from reporters fishing for information about the murders, and every time my back stair creaked I remembered Surgelato's suggestion that someone might be obsessed with killing editors-in-chief. It seemed a good idea to leave the hovel for a while.

I walked the few blocks to my parents' flat, missing the old head shops that had once flourished along Haight Street. Now everywhere you looked it was gourmet cookware and designer tennis shoes. Without the old splashes of psychedelia, Haight-Ashbury was just another drab neighborhood.

My parents' apartment, on the other hand, hadn't changed a bit. It still looked like a cross between a monastery and a radical left poster shop. The furnishings ranged from wood-framed canvas couches to gargantuan, incense-scented floor cushions. On the walls, Russian and Greek Orthodox icons nudged posters that screamed NICARAGUA FOR THE NICARAGUANS! and NO MORE VIETNAMS!

I went to my old room and dropped my duffel bag at

the foot of the bed, still unmade from my last stay. I spent most of that day wallowing in Jefferson Airplane and Cream records and admiring the Avalon Ballroom posters on my wall. (San Francisco posters no longer advertise concerts; they warn about AIDS and recommend "safe sex.")

I phoned Greg Parker's wife the next morning and found out from her sister that Greg still hadn't returned. I called the police to see what they were doing about it.

"And where have you been?" Don Surgelato demanded.

"I'm at my parents' house."

"Another hour and I'da got a warrant to kick your effing door in."

"My landlord would have blamed it on the Trilateral Commission." He thought Henry Kissinger and David Rockefeller were behind every ill that befell the city in general, and him in particular.

"The what? Didn't I tell you to check in with us if you planned to leave town?"

"You may have. But I happen to be in town."

There was a short silence. I don't think the lieutenant appreciated the distinction.

He snapped, "Address?"

"You're not coming here, are you?" There was a cloud of marijuana smoke in the living room.

"Address?"

I gave him my parents' address.

"No, we're not coming, not now anyway."

"Do you know where Greg Parker is?"

"No, I don't. Do you?"

"No."

"When did you last see Parker?"

I told him about our office-cleaning party.

"Did Parker say anything to you then—anything at all—to make you think he wanted to run off? About his wife, for instance?"

"No. Believe me, Greg Parker's not a rolling stone type of guy."

"Well, did he say anything that coulda made somebody nervous? Something about the murders?"

"He talked about his eczema."

"Nothing at all? No little thing?"

I knew I should tell him about the note in the manila envelope. "No."

"Well, call us if you think of something. In the meantime, I'd appreciate you not mentioning the possible incident to anyone."

The possible incident. I hoped Surgelato never wrote a law review article.

"Are you doing anything to find Greg?"

He snorted and hung up.

I paced around for a while, fretting. I decided to call the former owners of Clarence Day's properties, the ones on Susan Green's list. If I could find out why Susan had made that false will, it might be useful.

I located a business number in the White Pages for one of the two men on the list. When he answered the phone, I told him, "I'm calling for the State Bar of California. We're investigating possible infractions by Clarence Day of a rule prohibiting lawyers from purchasing property owned by their clients."

"I know your voice. Didn't you call me the other day?"

"I was confirming that you'd sold the property. Today I'm following up on that call."

"Who did you say you were?"

"The State Bar of California."

"Oh. Does Day know about this?"

"He requested the investigation to clear up the allegation against him."

"Oh. Well, I listed the property because it was either that or go into bankruptcy. And thank God Day bought it! Damn thing stayed on the market for weeks—and meanwhile my business was going down the toilet! Day was handling my affairs. He thought I ought to go ahead and do a Chapter 11 and hang on to the land, to tell the truth."

The other former owner, luckily, did not recognize my voice. He told me he'd been trying to work out "a seven-figure divorce settlement" with his wife at the time. He'd sold of some off his separate property to bribe her into letting him keep the community property house his kids loved so much ("Not many houses in San Fran with an Olympic pool, you know"). His wife had been "a hard-ass" about it for months, but then one day she'd shown signs of wavering. "If Day hadn't bought that piece-of-junk warehouse right then and there, cash money, she'd have changed her mind, what do you want to bet me?"

I thanked him and hung up, wondering if Susan Green had been trying to get Clarence Day disciplined or beatified.

I started to call Larry a couple of times. It was habit, I guess; I'd gotten used to talking to him around school. But Greg's disappearance made me nervous. I couldn't get his warning out of my mind: Investigate Tchielowicz. Besides, Tchielowicz was probably busy with his vestal girlfriend, drinking milk and listening to Up with People records.

I also considered calling Jake Whittsen. I might have ignored an affronted wife, but I decided a jealous girlfriend was the kind of double whammy I could live without.

I got stoned a lot, read all the romance novels hidden under my mother's bed, and sent cables to every group of Catholic American do-gooders in El Salvador, trying to track down my parents.

I didn't go back to my apartment until Christmas Eve.

20

AT SIX O'CLOCK sharp Gunnar Haas rang my doorbell.

I was wearing a long-sleeved red wool dress that was itchy as hell but looked great on me; I wanted Gunnar Haas' scalp on my belt.

He held out a small gift-wrapped package.

That was more like it. A girl gets sick of disapproval.

It was a little glass ornament, very pretty, of a unicorn. I smiled. "Thank you, professor. But do you know the legend? This little guy's come to the wrong place."

"Please call me Gunnar." He smiled too. Apparently he knew the legend.

Dean Sorenson did not seem surprised to see me at Gunnar's side. He was excessively gracious, in fact, calling me "dear girl" and introducing me to some fossilized district court judges as "the editor-in-chief of our marvelous law review." One of the hizzoners kept calling me "Miss Green," which showed that he read the law review but didn't read the newspapers.

I noticed a couple of professors staring at me; they turned hastily away when I met their gaze. A hawk-nosed criminal procedure professor was the exception. He weaved over to me and insisted that I "keep the police within the scope of their authority. They have no right to interfere with the legitimate operation of the law review, Miss, uh—"

"Jansson."

A portly evidence professor wheeled around to snap, "The *police* interfere! What about the lowlife who killed Susan Green? I suppose he *didn't* interfere!"

Around us, conversations stopped.

"Are you suggesting that the police use Rambo tactics to control crime?" The hawk-nosed professor tugged at his bow tie; sweat began to bead on his upper lip. "Are you suggesting that the Fourth Amendment doesn't apply to violent crime? That the innocent may be harassed so that the guilty—"

"Fourth Amendment my foot! Would you let your daughter enroll at Malhousie next year? What do you think will happen if this isn't cleared up by—"

"Enrollment is not the issue here!"

The dean stepped between them, clapping the evidence

professor on the back and enthusing, "Who's going to win the Rose Bowl, gentlemen? *That's* the issue!"

Gunnar took my elbow and began guiding me through the crowd toward the refreshment table. Along the way he murmured hellos to male colleagues and complimented female colleagues on their attire. Uniformed caterers thrust trays of stuffed mushrooms and tiny wontons in front of us, and we stopped a few times to exchange pleasantries with professors on the tenure committee. Gunnar introduced me as "the editor of law review, for which I am advisor." The professors seemed surprised Gunnar had a mere student in tow, but, as one magnanimously observed, "Editor-in-chief; I suppose that's quasi-professorial!" And Gunnar's point was not lost on them: he would help them get their articles into print—if they helped him achieve tenure.

It was half an hour before we made it to a massive dragon-legged table with an avalanche of Brie and pâté on it.

At arm's length from a crystal tub of punch (the kind you shouldn't light a match near) stood Professor Miles, already half gone at quarter past seven. By eight-thirty she'd be on her fanny. She always was. At last year's law review banquet they'd had to carry her out to her taxi. I guess teaching trusts and estates will do that to a person.

She lowered her eyelids and pruned up her mouth when she saw me. Gunnar greeted her and said wasn't it nice that I could join them. A bad-tempered drunk, she replied, "With what's been going on downstairs, I wonder Ms. Jansson has the heart for it."

Gunnar looked shocked to the marrow. I wanted to needle her, so I asked if she'd found Harold Scharr the day she'd claimed to be looking for him. I added, "Perhaps you meant to leave him a note; I noticed you were searching the desks." I'd already taken her damned class, what else could she do to me?

I was amply rewarded. Professor Miles blanched, swaying like a stalk of corn. Then she replied stiffly, "I don't recall the day you mean."

I mixed up my facts (I realized this later). "It was the day you came downstairs to complain about the accuracy of our editor's note."

Her eyes widened. "You mean the *inaccuracy*."

"What did I say?"

"Accuracy."

"Oh." Gunnar distracted me with a cup of punch, and I began to ogle the Brie.

I heard Professor Miles' bracelets jangling, and I looked up to find her stalking off, hipbones first, as usual.

Gunnar began describing an article he'd just written, about a unique Swedish statute. I feigned interest and encouraged him to bring it downstairs and let us consider it for our summer issue. He was up for tenure in the next academic year, and he needed to publish as many pieces as he possibly could.

Then I spotted Clarence and Jane Day glad-handing the faculty and looking about as happy and charming as two people can look. He kept his arm around her small, sequined shoulders, and she periodically turned to him with a look of adoration. In less than a year, she'd probably be our state attorney general, and the faculty was all but curtseying to her. They treated her husband with the exaggerated deference law professors always display toward lawyers who have proven their virility in the courtroom.

I'd never talked to Clarence Day, and after my conversation with Mrs. Koenig, I was curious about him. Gunnar was chatting with a visiting professor, so I slipped away to join the Days' entourage.

Clarence Day was asked about his latest case, which he'd won to the tune of sixty million—twenty-five for him and thirty-five for the client. I worked my way closer to him.

I said, "I watched you argue the Koenig case a few years back. I was surprised the jury found for Walter Bonomini."

There was a second of silence as Day tried to place me; maybe that was natural—who wants to discuss a losing case with a stranger? But his wife's reaction was something else. Her lapis-blue eyes opened wide, then narrowed. She spilled her drink down the front of her gorgeous gown, and there was much oh-noing and offering of napkins. Clarence Day became part of the minor melee, and everyone forgot I'd said anything.

But one thing was certain: Jane Day didn't want her husband discussing the Koenig case.

I spent the rest of the party making legal small talk with bored professors and trying not to be offended by their air of noblesse oblige.

Gunnar Haas, with tenure on his mind, wasn't ready to leave until most of the others had said goodbye and the dean stood at his Chinese table stifling yawns.

I was glad to climb back into Gunnar's Alfa Romeo and head for home.

Gunnar came in with me, and I explained about the herpes, swearing to him it was not active.

Nevertheless, he mumbled something about "safe sex,"

making it sound like a matter of principle. He told me he preferred to use a "precaution." Interesting that he'd brought one, I thought.

We spent a disappointing hour together. I guess sex is like conversation. It's who you're with, not what you're doing.

We went to a restaurant afterward, a crowded little place on the avenues that Gunnar said had been highly recommended to him. We were halfway through our pasta, having one of those strained aftermath conversations, when I saw Melissa Whittsen near the door. She was slipping on a cashmere coat. Helping her with it, and receiving for his trouble a Mona Lisa smile, was Clarence Day.

Clarence fucking Day.

I thought about the Days for hours that night, tossing in my bed, wishing morning would come so I could call Tchielowicz.

But I had other things on my mind Christmas morning. I got a response to one of the cables I'd sent to El Salvador. It read, "Mother sick. Visa problems. Father says shake Silvio's tree."

Silvio Bernstein was our congressman. He'd grown up with my dad and was considered a liberal—certainly more liberal than most of his constituents, who'd voted him in by voting the incumbent out. But Silvio was currently running for reelection, and to read his latest flyers you'd think he and Ronald Reagan had been cloned from the same horse's behind.

The cable scared me to death, and I spent the day on the phone to everyone I could think of who might know how to find Silvio and help me shake his tree.

In fact, I spent most of the following week doing that. Nothing else seemed very important.

21

I DIDN'T BREATHE easy until the day spring semester classes began. I'd left the law review's phone number with Silvio's office, and I got a call there from his aide.

"Everything's okay now," he boomed heartily. "We have word that your mother is well and that your parents are out of El Salvador and safe in Honduras."

Safe in Honduras—that's a laugh. I've been there. Hondurans aren't safe in Honduras. But it was an improvement over El Salvador; at least interfering liberals weren't routinely murdered.

My peace of mind partially restored, I started thinking about Clarence Day again, about seeing him with Melissa Whittsen. I knew Tchielowicz would be interested, but I hadn't seen him around school.

I decided to leave him a note.

The day of our office cleaning we'd thrown away class notes and outlines, but we'd saved rejected manuscripts, stacking them typed-side down to use as scratch paper. I grabbed a page off the pile and scrawled a message for Tchielowicz to meet me for lunch. I slipped it face down into his mailbox, one of many short, wide cubbyholes near the door. That's when I noticed what was written on the other side.

It was a footnoted quotation in a foreign language. There was nothing necessarily odd about that; authors love to show they're multilingual. But the language was Scandinavian—it was studded with those diagonally slashed o's.

I pulled the sheet back out of Tchielowicz's cubbyhole, skimming the text. It was page six of a manuscript about a Swedish statute. In fact, it was page six of the manuscript Gunnar Haas had described at the dean's cocktail party.

Gunnar had told me it was still being typed, that he'd bring it downstairs as soon as it was done.

But the pile of scratch paper had been assembled more than a week before the dean's party. It looked as though Gunnar Haas had already brought the article downstairs once.

I riffled through the rest of the scrap pile but found no more of the manuscript. Either Gunnar Haas had returned to retrieve it or the police had removed it in the course of their homicide investigation.

I crossed into the inner office and sat at my old desk, rubbing a bit of sheen onto the scrubbed surface. I couldn't remember a time, before the murders, when the inner office hadn't been crowded with editors rewriting articles, proofing galleys, groaning over convoluted legalisms. Now it was so quiet I could hear engines rev and car doors slam in the faculty garage.

I picked up the telephone and called the cops. "This is

the editor-in-chief of the *Malhousie Law Review*. You took an article into evidence, the article you found on Susan Green's desk. I need it back, for our summer issue.''

I was switched to Homicide. "I'm sorry, we can't release evidence.''

"Can I talk to Lieutenant Surgelato?''

A woman came on the line. "Evidence.''

I repeated my set piece, adding, "Will you at least confirm for our editorial records that you do have Professor Haas' article?''

"Who did you say you were?'' Her tone was suspicious.

"Editor-in-chief of—''

A click, and I was cast into the limbo of hold.

Two slow minutes later, Don Surgelato came on the line. "Miss Jansson, what can I do for you?'' He spoke with the studied huskiness of a man saying, "Hey cutie, wanna—?''

I told him what I wanted.

"We made a mess of your office, and I'm sorry about that. But you look around, and I'm sure you'll find this article by—Haw, did you say?''

"It's not in your evidence locker?''

"I can't discuss that. But you look around your office; you'll probably find it somewhere.''

I hung up, went back to the outer office to brave a cup of coffee.

If the police hadn't taken Gunnar Haas' manuscript out of the office, then Gunnar had come downstairs and retrieved it (all but page six) before our office cleaning.

Why? And why had he told me the article was still unfinished?

Harold Scharr came in with anorexic Hatty. "You look

like thunder,'' he observed, wincing at the state of my hair.

"Why the hell is everyone lying to me? Why's everyone sneaking around here?''

Harold rubbed an imaginary smudge from his cufflink, remarking to Hatty, "Maybe we should have called first.''

Hatty wasn't one to enjoy a quip at the best of times. That day, she was coming unraveled. The laces of her peasant dress were untied, her honey-blond curls had tumbled free of her Alice headband, and her China doll face showed splotches of hysterical pink. "I just heard about Greg Parker. Why haven't you called a staff meeting? We should disband before someone else gets hurt!'' She jerked her hands at the command of some invisible puppeteer. "Why are you still giving us articles? We should—''

"Stop the presses after eighty-eight years? You think the faculty's going to let a little murder affect production of the school's precious law review?''

Mad-as-a-Hatty obviously didn't understand the illogical chauvinism "their'' law review inspired in the faculty. If we fell a goddam week behind schedule they were all over us, grousing about our reputation.

Hatty's head began to shake with a life of its own. "This makes three murders, Willa!''

Harold backed away, startled. "Don't add Greg to the body count! We don't know—''

"—and I won't stay! I won't stay here with a crazy person running around!''

I refrained from making the obvious observation. "Look, Hatty, I know, I know, it's terrible. But we really need you. Do your work at home if you like.''

She turned and began to weep on Harold's lapel. Harold

patted her curls, muttering wistfully, "My new Bill Blass."

Another group of editors came in, looking somber. When they saw Hatty, they averted their eyes. We had a brief, unenthusiastic conference about some manuscripts, and they left. No one wanted to dawdle over coffee in the outer office anymore.

Harold sat Hatty down and soothed her as she babbled tearfully about the police upsetting her grandmother, about the state bar adding an oral section to the bar exam, and especially about men on the streetcar trying to touch her. Harold put himself and his new Datsun sports car at her disposal, but Hatty continued her tirade, complaining that her interviews weren't going well and that everyone but her was finding a job. Harold maintained a sympathetic air and sneaked glances at his wristwatch.

I missed my appellate procedure class because some other editors came in to stow their raquetball gear and indulge in morbid speculation about Greg, which I did my best to quash.

There were maybe eight of us collected on the couches alternately brooding about Greg and the bar exam when Jane Day popped her head in and looked around. She spotted me and beckoned. I joined her in the drafty hall-way.

She extended a cool hand, and I shook it, wondering how long it had taken the pearl on her finger to crush its unlucky shellmate.

Lady Jane's hair was tidily chignoned despite a fierce January wind, her skin had the opalescence of perfect makeup, her lavender linen suit showed no ghost of a wrinkle, and her high heels exactly matched the beige lace of her blouse. It should have cost money just to look at her.

"So nice to see you again, Miss uh—"

It took me a second to answer, "Jansson." I was getting used to "Miss Uh."

"I hear that one of your editors is missing."

I nodded.

Jane Day drew her straight brows together, but not enough to encourage worry lines. "How alarming! Do you know anything about it?"

"No. Greg Parker came to the law review office, then he disappeared. That's all I know."

"Did you see him here?"

I was too busy admiring her suit to watch my big mouth. "No, he left me a note."

She pounced on this. "A note? What about?"

"Nothing. A case. The security guard doesn't remember seeing him, but someone might have opened the basement door for him if he came in through the garage."

"Is there a basement door? I've always gone around to the front when I've parked down here."

I wanted to say, "Then you must be blind as a bat." Instead, I pointed down the hall to the door.

I heard footsteps and turned to see Mary West coming down the stairs, prominent chin held high. She stopped when she reached the storage room door. "Where the hell is Jake Whittsen?" she demanded, looking through us. "I've got something to say to him."

"Mary, leave it alone. What's the—"

"Oh don't give me any of your bullshit!" She shoved past me into the office, calling behind her, "Just leave me the fuck alone, because I've got the balls to tell the truth, even if you and Melissa don't.''

I turned back to Jane Day and found her looking after Mary with stern, even angry, disapproval. I wondered what she'd do if I told her Clarence had spent Christmas Eve with the aforementioned Melissa. It was wonderfully ironic, and I began to feel a little better.

Jane Day inquired politely about my job prospects, and I told her I planned to work for Julian Warneke. She reacted like a woman discovering a dog pie on her shoe. But she gave me an idea.

When I went back into the office, Mary was perched on an arm of the sagging Naugahyde couch, repeating, and no doubt crudely paraphrasing, Melissa's query, "Has every woman in the office been screwing Jake?"

Harold looked embarrassed. He didn't much care for gossip; he usually faded into the background when other editors unsheathed their claws. Unfortunately for him, his reticence made him a sought-after confidant, as the tear stains on his lapel demonstrated.

Hatty sat there blinking her big, wet eyes at Mary; she was too gone on her own problems to care about anyone else's.

The other editors were stifling smiles and pretending to peruse literature about the nine-week bar review course we'd have to endure after spring finals.

I stayed in the outer office just long enough to snatch the graffitoed interview schedule off the wall above the couch. Then I fled into the inner office and slammed the door.

I phoned the placement office, reaching a boosterish

woman who gave seminars on "Pepping up Your Résumé!!"

"Is it too late for me to get an interview with Wailes, Roth?" Wailes, Roth, Fotheringham & Beck was the firm of choice for robber barons, multinational corporations, and major banks. According to Larry Tchielowicz (via Greg Parker), that Wall Street firm had offered John Hancock Henderson a job.

"Their representative is on campus tomorrow, if that's what you mean. This is the first year they've bothered with us, to tell the truth." The woman laughed, but she sounded offended. "Their appointments have been set for two months now, though. Top five percent and—"

"Law review, I know. Could they possibly squeeze me in?"

"I'd like to help you out, honey, really, but we gave them a stack of résumés, and it was all we could do to get them to interview four people—and the three they're interviewing tomorrow are at the very top of the class—"

"Maybe they'll see me if you tell them I'm editor-in-chief of the law review."

There was a short silence. "I thought Susan Green—"

"Acting editor. I used to be senior articles editor. And I think I'm still in the top five." Federal income tax grades had yet to be posted. "If I run my résumé over, will you give it to them?"

"I'm supposed to follow the procedure, Ms.—?"

"Jansson."

"But I'll do what I can."

I hung up, studying the schedule I'd pulled off the wall. Wailes, Roth would be interviewing one of our technical editors in the morning and two of our articles editors, including Jake Whittsen, that afternoon. The interviewers appeared to have some dead time before lunch. Maybe they'd see me then.

Once in the interview room, I might be able to discover whether Wailes, Roth had extended John Henderson a job offer. If they had, Henderson had certainly accepted—I couldn't see him declining so prestigious and remunerative an offer. In which case, why had he told Martin Relke he planned to work for Clarence Day?

I did a mental inventory of my wardrobe (no lavender linen suits, alas). I was probably the only third-year law student at Malhousie who still felt itchy and constricted in a business suit. But I supposed I could pass for a nascent reactionary in my blue three-piece. And it would definitely be interesting, interviewing for the piggiest firm on The Street.

I leaned back in my chair, murmuring, "Willa Jansson, Republican for a day."

A voice said, "Pardon?"

I turned to find Jake Whittsen standing in the doorway. I'd forgotten how handsome he was, how self-contained he seemed with his expressionless face and black-coffee eyes. He reminded me of that famous portrait of Sitting Bull, dignity transcendent.

"Come in, Jake. Close the door."

Maybe that was the wrong thing to say. He looked alarmed, as if he feared I'd jump at his fly.

"Have you talked to Mary?" He neither met my eye nor closed the door.

"She's not out there now?"

He shook his head.

"You're lucky! Yes, I've talked to her. You have too, I take it."

"Every goddam day. I sure didn't bargain for this from Modern Mary!"

Another wonderful irony.

"She acts so tough, like a little sex is nothing, you know. And then, wham, she decides she's in love—doesn't know a thing about me, or want to, but she's knitting goddam baby booties! Whatever happened to free love?"

"Went the way of the free lunch, I guess. I'm really sorry about Melissa. About that night."

If I hadn't been sure before, the pain in his eyes would have made it unmistakably clear that this was a man who loved his wife.

"Look, Jake, are you sure she's . . . you know?"

The line of his mouth and jaw grew bitter. "I'm sure."

"She told you?"

I swear this happened. You may think it's too small a thing to notice, or too little upon which to base a conclusion, but when I asked Jake that question, he looked right at the chair in the corner. Greg Parker used to sit in that chair. We never did give Greg a desk of his own because he drove us all crazy with his old-ladyish snooping, but he got back at us by sitting in the inner office all the time anyway, in the corner near the bookcase. At that moment, I'd have bet my last dollar that Nosy Parker had been the one to squeal on Melissa.

"Jake, I don't mean to pry, but do you know who Melissa's been seeing?"

He did not seem inclined to answer me. He left the room abruptly, like a man who'd rather die than cry in public.

22

I RAN UP to the library to take a look at a case I knew an author had misinterpreted. The author, a hot dog professor at Boalt Hall, had split hairs, chopped words from unrelated quotations, and spliced together unlike legal rulings to conclude that purse snatchers have a duty to take good care of their illicit handbags. Anything to get tenure, I guess.

There was a crowd of people in the cement-walled library lobby. They were facing the locked safety-glass display cases on either side of the library doors.

It didn't take a girl detective to figure out what it meant: Fall semester grades had been posted.

I elbowed nearer to the front and was quickly infected with the same rapt apprehension I saw on my classmates' faces. The grades were organized by course name and listed according to the last four digits of our social security numbers. The dean figured this would eliminate grade comparing, but students managed to discover their classmates' "exam numbers" by cross-referencing to other classes their targets had taken.

One of the cafeteria pinball morons shouted across the lobby, "Hey, 8465, looks like you blew corporations, buddy!" Beside him, a doe-eyed first-year student burst into tears. Behind me, relieved sighs and distressed profanity could be heard with equal frequency. And I spotted the grade list for federal income tax.

A 78, the lowest possible B; not bad for someone who didn't understand depreciation, but bye-bye top five. I checked my other grades, which were what I expected, then sidled toward the library doors. I nudged past Hatty McPherson, but she didn't notice me; her eyes were riveted to a grade list, her face frozen with shock. She shook her head, whispering, "No, no, no." A true friend would have stopped to comfort her. I kept on going.

Malhousie's library is one big room with stacks along the walls and a dozen big tables clustered in the middle. A mezzanine balcony stretches all the way around. It's usually filled with cabbage-brained jocks sitting along the rail in creaky carrels, ogling the first-year women downstairs. It's the smoking section, and habit usually takes me up there.

I took a carrel near a wall of law reviews, gritted my teeth, and did a little editing. (I'd never thought of a purse snatcher as a "voluntary bailor" before; I probably never will again.) It was difficult to concentrate. I couldn't stop thinking about Jane Day. The law review had survived eighty-eight years of student editors, but Jane Day was the only one still making sentimental journeys to the office. I glanced at the wall of law reviews and did some mental calculation. Jane Day was a young woman, maybe ten years older than me. Assuming she'd started law school right after college, she'd have graduated from Malhousie fifteen years ago, give or take a few years.

She said she'd been on law review; that meant she'd published an article. I pulled down some old *Malhousie Law Reviews* and flipped through the tables of contents. In a fifteen-year-old review, I found an article by Jane Bartlett, which I knew from her campaign literature was Lady Jane's maiden name. Like Susan Green's article, Jane Bartlett's was about campaign financing laws, though it dealt of necessity with the early precursors of the current laws. Lady Jane's political aspirations were obviously not of recent origin.

The editor's note preceding her article listed a half-dozen ambitious accomplishments, among them aide to a state senator, research assistant to two professors, and student representative on the moot court board; I wondered when Jane Bartlett had found the time to write so long an article.

I remembered Lady Jane fingering the filed drafts of Susan Green's manuscript and decided to compare the two articles. I pulled down the latest issue of the review and skimmed Susan's article. It contained no reference to Jane Bartlett's article, though Susan must have encountered it in her research. I supposed the earlier article was too dated to warrant discussion, though Susan should at least have cited it in a footnote, for thoroughness' sake.

I began to feel increasingly uncomfortable, as though someone were watching me. I looked down into the main room. There weren't many students studying down there, mostly second-years, getting started on articles they hoped would win them editorial positions. None showed the slightest interest in me.

Before putting away Lady Jane's article, I flipped to the

masthead. I was surprised to find Jane Bartlett listed as executive editor. Next to editor-in-chief, that was the most time-consuming position on the staff; Lady Jane had certainly been a busy law student.

I noticed Virginia Miles was listed as faculty advisor.

Hours before Susan Green's murder, Professor Miles had railed at her about some damned editor's note. A week later, the professor had been asking odd questions about the law review and snooping around the office.

I became curious about the editor's note. I took the latest issue of the review back to my carrel and looked up the professor's article. An italicized sentence above the first footnote summarized Virginia Miles' accomplishments: a bachelor's degree from Swarthmore, a law degree from Yale, a legal masters and doctorate from Columbia, and two research prizes, neither of them recent.

I skimmed the footnotes until I found the inevitable reference to one of the professor's own, earlier articles, also in a *Malhousie Law Review*. I found the review, looked up the article, and skimmed that editor's note. It included a nonlegal masters and doctorate that the latter had not. Either Susan Green had shortened Professors Miles' list of credits for editorial economy or she'd done some research and found the two degrees to be bogus.

Tchielowicz's voice startled me. "Not a churchgoer, are you?"

"Larry!" I wheeled around, happier than I had reason to be.

He smiled, and I felt myself blush. "I didn't see you in church Christmas Eve."

"Christmas Eve? That was weeks ago." I was experiencing a surge of pride at how broad his chest was, how discerning his expression. Looking up at him, I began to realize what a fool I was.

"There was a beautiful midnight service at Peter and Paul's—you wouldn't know. The choir is extraordinary for a group of amateurs. They have a strong soprano section, some interesting people singing. Including Jane Day. She has a very pretty voice. I thought of you."

"Jane Day sang at the midnight service Christmas Eve?"

"Whoa—this is an icebreaker, not a clue."

"At the midnight service! No, I wasn't there, and I'll tell you who else wasn't!" I lowered my voice, "Her husband!"

Larry pulled up a chair from a neighboring carrel, and we sat down. I told him about seeing Clarence Day with Melissa Whittsen Christmas Eve.

"Where were you?"

"Café Riggio, on Geary. The man I was with—" I stopped, feeling foolishly coy. "I was with Gunnar Haas."

That brought a quick frown to Larry's face.

"He took me to Dean Sorenson's cocktail party. Then afterward he said he'd heard about this restaurant—I wonder if Clarence Day recommended it."

"Day was at the cocktail party?"

"Yes—and when I asked him about the Koenig case, Lady Jane spilled a drink all over herself!"

"Sounds like you were a charming guest." He traced a pattern on the carrel's marred surface.

"The point is, Day and Melissa! You don't spend Christmas Eve with someone unless you're romantically—"

"Any word from Parker yet?"

I hesitated, visualizing the neatly typed note I'd found on my desk.

He gripped my shoulder. "What's up? Bad news?"

"Nothing's up. They haven't found him."

He scrutinized my face, his blue eyes narrowed. "Something's on your mind, Nancy Drew. Out with it."

I wondered again, how much damage could a man do with a baseball bat? "The afternoon we came here to call Greg—" I looked away.

He released my shoulder. "Yes, a morning of revelations. Go on."

"When Mary West came in, I was picking up an envelope I found on my desk. I forgot I had it till I got home."

"And?"

"It was a note. I think Greg left it for me."

His expression grew guarded. "Greg did? Have you told the police?"

"No. It was anonymous. It was about you, Larry."

His lips curled cynically. "Is that so?"

"It said you had a criminal record." I could feel the balcony rails against my back. I'm not sure why, but I decided to lie. "That's all it said."

"Well. How disappointing that your anonymous note wasn't more explicit."

It took a moment for the implication to sink in: He was accusing me of trying to trick more information out of him. "Fuck you, Larry!"

"Me and Gunnar Haas and Jake Whittsen, huh?"

I stood up, my chair clattering against the rails. "Oh, do my morals offend you? You're a real traditional-values,

button-down kind of guy, aren't you? Or I should say, you
are *now*!''

"Jesus, Willa, keep your voice down!" He pushed his
chair away from the carrel, farther from me. "What I did,
I paid for! It's not something I like to talk about, okay?"

"You've made that plenty clear—and insulted me in the
bargain!"

"Look, I didn't mean—"

"I thought you should know Greg Parker found out
about it. That's all." I glanced over the rail. Beneath me,
Virginia Miles froze in the act of handing an envelope to
Harold Scharr. Both looked up at me.

I continued more quietly. "So if you'll excuse me, I'll
remove my immoral self from your presence."

As I walked past him, he took hold of my wrist. "Willa,
I'm sorry. What you do is none of my damn business."

I jerked my wrist free and walked away.

23

I WAS NO Jane Day; that was apparent to me when I saw
my reflection in the placement office window. My blue

wool suit looked linty and off-the-rack, and a January gale had made my hair look like I'd taken a Cuisinart to it.

I did what I could with it and presented myself to the buxom redhead at the front desk. Behind her, a poster urged me to "put the *Zoom* back in résumé!" "Will Wailes, Roth see me?"

The woman looked me over, leaning across the desk to brush lint off my sleeve. "Yes." She pointed to the interview room where Lieutenant Surgelato had bedroom-eyed me. "But you're late. I told them eleven."

It was eleven-ten. Goddam Hayes Street bus driver had stopped to chase a purse snatcher (or should I say a "voluntary bailor"?) through the projects. Bus drivers aren't usually so chivalrous, but the purse had been his own.

I tapped at the interview room door, and was instructed, in the driest of tones, to enter.

There were two of them, middle-aged men who looked like they'd just stepped out of coffins. The one on the left wore a suit so gray it might as well have been black. He was skinny, pale, stooped over, with small glasses and a large nose. The one on the right wore a suit so blue it might as well have been black. He was stout, pale, and horn-rimmed, with prep school and Republican Central Committee written all over him. Each wore a deep red tie; on them, the ties seemed almost wild.

I smiled. In response, they did something with their faces. It looked like they'd bitten into sour plums. Maybe that's how they smile on Wall Street.

"Pleas sit down, Miss uh—" The stout one glanced at my résumé.

"Jansson."

The other one leaned back in his gouged wooden chair

and looked me over. "I see you're law review, Miss Jansson."

L'état, c'est moi. "Yes. I imagine you were, also."

"Columbia," he informed me, lowering his eyelids a pompous fraction. "My colleague here was Yale."

"Both of them excellent reviews," I said, with a laudably straight face.

Columbia sniffed. "Malhousie's had a symposium or two these last few years; you're getting there, I think."

"Why thank you."

"I see you graduated from Stanford," Yale observed, frowning at my résumé. "What was your major?"

"Latin American Literature."

He blinked at me. "Oh, do they have—?"

"Books? Yes, they do. A surprising number."

"Of course, huh, huh. Well, can you tell us why you want to join Wailes, Roth?"

"A friend of mine was very interested in working for you. He said many complimentary things about your—"

Columbia and Yale exchanged glances.

"John Henderson," I concluded. "Did you meet him when he visited your New York office?"

Columbia nodded. Neither man looked at me.

"I believe your firm made him an offer."

Yale looked especially uncomfortable. "It's too bad about the publicity," he ventured. "I imagine it's proving a serious obstacle to all of you on the review."

"An obstacle?"

"In terms of employment options."

Columbia shot him a warning glance, interjecting, "Perhaps we can tell you a bit about Wailes. We are competitive with all the major''—he stressed major— ''New York firms. Of course, you're aware of the salary war.''

I shook my head.

''Cravath, Swaine raised first-year associate salaries to sixty-five.'' He bit into the sour plum again. ''We're pleased to match that, of course.''

I almost fell off my chair: sixty-five grand a year! Forty-three thousand more than Julian Warneke would be paying me. No wonder Henderson had wanted to work on The Street.

Columbia continued, ''It may take a few months for the increase to go into effect; the machinery moves rather slowly at firms of our—'' he cast about for the proper word.

''Magnitude? John Henderson told me a little about your practice. He was certainly looking forward to working for you.''

Again the two men exchanged glances.

''I'm sorry, do I have it wrong? Didn't you make John an offer?''

''I believe we may have,'' Yale said stiffly.

And Columbia added, ''We began the interview process before any of this . . . *imbroglio* began.''

The men were studying the table top. I finally realized what they were telling me. No wonder Hatty McPherson was having a hard time finding a job.

''I appreciate your position, gentlemen.'' I stood up, noticing an accordian of wrinkles in my skirt. ''I won't expect to hear from you before this 'imbroglio' has been cleared up.''

24

FOR SOME INCOMPREHENSIBLE reason, Mary West appointed herself a one-woman Find Greg Parker Committee. We all wanted to find Greg, but Mary, who used to say he looked like a limp dick, began xeroxing enlargements of his photograph and taping them to phone booths. On each enlargement, she listed the law review's phone numbers, pleading: "Please [double underlined] call if you've seen this man since December 17th."

The police had given up trying to keep the "possible incident" a secret, and Greg's picture had gone out on the wire services. Brown-shirted security guards now prowled Malhousie's corridors, escorting out reporters and others who couldn't produce either student ID or a bar association membership card. Nevertheless, I had another visit from the tentative young reporter who'd come to see me about Susan Green a couple of months earlier.

He said (pause), "Remember me? Manuel Boyd, *San Francisco Express*?"

I yawned. I'd been up most of the night learning, for my creditors' rights class, how to squeeze money out of bankrupt debtors. (Julian Warneke had advised me to "know the enemy.") "Sure, come in."

Boyd looked around the inner office, his expression intent. I looked around, too; the office seemed overly tidy and underused, all its mess concentrated on my desk.

"I'd like to do a profile of Gregory Parker." His long nose twitched, and he glanced at me, looking quickly away. "You knew him fairly well?"

"Not really." More to the point, I didn't want to offend his relatives with my honest opinion.

He was squinting at the bookcases, scanning the titles. I looked at the books, too, but they didn't tell me anything. "What kind of activities did Parker like?"

"Water-skiing and mountain climbing."

Manuel Boyd looked startled; he looked me in the eye, his mouth opening and closing.

I laughed. "You've already talked to a few people."

He nodded.

"I'm not really sure what he liked to do. I think he did church group kinds of things. Are you really here to ask me about Greg?"

Manuel Boyd had a quick spark of a smile, there and gone before you had a chance to take a look at it. "Partly. And partly to put myself at your service."

It was my turn to be surprised. "Doing what?"

He fingered the spiral of his notebook. "Anything you want to ask me? I've been talking to just about everyone in San Francisco who knows Greg Parker."

"Oh." I leaned back in my chair and looked at Manuel Boyd. There was a suggestion of Salvation Army about his shiny corduroy jacket and badly knotted tie. "You're doing this for the *Express*?"

He nodded, looking up at the sweating maze of overhead pipes.

"Do they pay you?"

He looked back down, shaking his head. "But somebody will, if I add a couple more good pieces to my portfolio."

"What do you do for money in the meantime?"

"Anything temporary. Right now I fill vending machines." He pointed to the outer office, and I noticed a stack of cardboard boxes, no doubt filled with stale crackers and petrified cookies. "That's how I got past security."

"Well, there is one thing you could tell me: Did Greg know anybody in Indiana?"

"Not that I heard about."

I motioned for him to sit at Susan's desk, and I rolled my chair closer. "You're a reporter, you're trained to find out things: If you wanted to know whether someone had a juvenile record—closed file—how would you do it?"

"Find out where they used to live, get hold of someone who knew 'em, and ask. People remember that kind of thing."

I mulled this over, glancing at the telephone.

Manuel Boyd's smile came and went. "Why do you ask?"

"Nothing to do with Greg."

"Don't get mad, but I don't believe you."

He was looking me in the eye; I was the one who looked away this time. "I've got to go to class now."

Boyd nodded, pulling a checkbook out of his jacket pocket. He tore out a deposit slip and handed it to me. "Name, phone number, and address," he observed, tapping the lefthand corner. "It's as good as a business card, and God knows I never use them up."

I noticed the address. "You don't live far from me."

"Great neighborhood for over-priced gelato," he observed with disgust.

When he left, I went upstairs to the business office and told the secretary I was afraid some of my editors had been making personal long-distance calls on law review phones. I asked for a copy of our phone bills and made a pest of myself till I got them. Then I went back down to the office, glad for once to find it deserted. I looked through the bills till I found an Indiana phone number. I dialed it.

"Saint Anne's," said a weary voice.

So, the nosy bastard had phoned Larry's orphanage!

"Hi. I'm following up on a phone call made to you last month by Gregory Parker."

"Don't know the name. What was it in regards to?"

"One of your former charges, Lawrence Tchielowicz."

The voice grew cautious. "I didn't talk to no Gregory Parker."

"Oh, I'm sorry. It must have been someone else from this office then."

"You take my advice and give Larry that job. He was a fine boy, and what he done nobody could blame him for!"

"Would you mind telling me what happened?"

"I told that Mr. Henderson, any man that molests a child's got it coming as far as I'm concerned. I'm only sorry we didn't know what kind of man we was hiring! He was molesting the little boys, too, you know. I told

Mr. Henderson, Conrad Hall got what was coming to him!"

Henderson! That snake in the grass! "We were just concerned because we thought if it was really like that, they'd have acquitted Lar—Mr. Tchielowicz."

"They said he waited too long to do it, so it wasn't no self-defense. But you know boys. They brood on these things. At first they're ashamed, then they get to brooding. You take my advice, miss. You give Larry a chance!"

"Just one more thing, this, this Mr. Hall, was he badly hurt?" I waited, eyes closed. "Hello? Are you there?"

"He died." Her voice had grown troubled. "But you see, Larry was half out of his mind, he didn't know his own strength."

I rang off, wishing I hadn't called. Maybe Conrad Hall did have it coming—probably he did—but I'd rather not have known that Larry Tchielowicz was capable of murder.

25

CALLED SEVERAL editorial meetings that week. We were racing to get our fourth and final issue to press, and that involved the usual conferring, wheedling, threatening, and gossiping.

Gunnar Haas finally brought me his article on the Swedish statute. I flipped through it immediately: there was page six, neatly in place and identical to the one I'd slipped into Larry's cubbyhole.

Gunnar watched warily.

"Just checking the length," I explained casually. "It looks interesting."

I promised to make room for it in our summer issue, and Gunnar offered to buy me dinner. At his suggestion, we went to an obscure, half-empty little place way out on the avenues. I didn't blame him for wanting to avoid gossip about dating a student.

Over dessert, I asked him what he'd discussed with Susan Green the day she'd been murdered.

Gunnar kept his eyes on his cheesecake, his close-shaven cheeks growing pale. "I do not recall having spoken with Miss Green that day."

"I saw you go into the office to pick up a couple of law reviews. They were stacked near Susan's desk, and Susan was sitting right there."

"Perhaps I did speak with her, then. But it is two months now since poor Susan—" He put down his fork, pushing his dessert plate away. "So young and intelligent—" He swallowed, covering his mouth with a sensitive hand.

I didn't know why Gunnar Haas had lied to me about his manuscript, but I couldn't see him smashing in Susan's head. Unlike Larry Tchielowicz, he seemed too gentle to be capable of murder.

And unlike Larry Tchielowicz, he didn't laugh much, and he didn't make me laugh.

When he took me home, I used the modern version of the headache excuse. I told him the virus was active.

26

I FOUND MARY West alone in the outer office. She was curled up on the couch, head thrown back, face wet with tears. Beside her was a Macy's bag, open like a cornucopia. Several bulky sweaters—a departure from Mary's usual cling-to-show-all style—spilled from the bag.

I approached her with caution. "What's wrong?"

She shook her head.

"I wish you'd bury the hatchet, Mary. I haven't even shaken Jake's hand since I found out how you feel about him."

"That asshole."

"Is he what this is all about?"

"He doesn't deserve tears. If he wants to carry a torch for her, she can shit on him with my blessing!"

Mine too, if it meant that Mary would stop assassinating my character to anyone who'd listen.

For the first time in weeks, Mary looked at me without enmity. ''She's been at her brother's in Alaska since Christmas, and she might as well have cut it off and taken it with her. Why the hell do nice men always get hung up on ball breakers?''

''Does Jake know who Melissa's been seeing?''

''That's what I goddam don't get: He knows she screwed around on him!'' She blotted her tears with an impatient sleeve. ''He saw a picture of her and her boyfriend together at a party. When she was supposed to be out of town!''

''Who was she with?''

''Jake wouldn't say.''

''Who showed him the picture?''

She frowned at her damp sleeve. ''I don't know.''

''Does he still have it?''

''What difference does it make?''

''None.'' But I'd have bet commercial paper that the photograph caught Melissa Whittsen with Clarence Day. I remembered Jake's glance at Parker's chair when I'd asked how he knew Melissa'd been unfaithful. Nosy Greg Parker had shown the photo to Jake. What else could it mean?

The question was, where had Parker gotten the picture? He'd sifted through our desks regularly. From whose had he extracted the snapshot? Henderson's? Had Henderson been on some kind of campaign to discover the skeletons in all our closets?

If so, it was clear someone hadn't much liked it.

I got up to answer the phone, hoping it was Silvio Bernstein with more news about my parents. It wasn't. It was Lieutenant Surgelato.

Greg Parker's body had washed up on a beach just south of Pacifica.

27

THE HOMICIDE DIVISION is on the fourth floor of the Hall of Justice, a suitably somber six-story building in a neighborhood of warehouses and freeway exits. If I'd spent one more minute in Lieutenant Surgelato's office, we'd have been obligated to begin exchanging Christmas cards. Worst of all, the lieutenant was engaging in torture; he was smoking in front of me.

"Suicide," he suggested for the hundredth time, stubbing out another Kool.

"Greg didn't kill anybody. Why should he commit suicide?"

"You know for a fact he didn't kill anybody? You know who did, maybe?"

I dragged my fingers through my bangs. "No. I reiterate: I don't know who killed Susan or Henderson—or Greg Parker."

"So tell me what you haven't told me yet. I know there's something." He tapped another Kool from the pack.

"I didn't know Greg very well—only through law review. Here, let me have one of those. No, never mind." On the wall opposite me, among the commendations, plaques, and diplomas, was a photograph of football players pouring champagne over Surgelato's head; I wished I could do the same.

"You knew Parker well enough. You knew Henderson. You knew Susan Green." Surgelato lowered his wide bottom onto a tidy desk and frowned till his continuous, mustache-thick brow bristled. "Greg Parker: what do you think of when I say the name?"

"Cigarettes."

He leaned forward expectantly, his cologne mingling with smoke to smell like a pool hall.

"That's what I think about, no matter whose name you say."

"Adjectives: fat, sexy, funny—what? What adjectives go with the name Greg Parker?"

"Nosy. Clammy. Icky. Straitlaced. I don't know."

"Let's work on nosy. Examples?"

I should have told Surgelato about the anonymous note. Henderson, not Parker, had phoned Larry's orphanage; that meant Parker had learned the secret secondhand, either by eavesdropping on John or by snooping through his desk.

I chose instead to tell the lieutenant about the sealed birthday card in my desk drawer. "When I came back from my conveyancing class, Greg wished me happy birthday."

"Nosy, okay. Who did it bug? Who did it get to?"

"John Henderson. Everything got to John Henderson. He was our office prima donna, he used to go around apologizing for not being at Yale or Stanford Law. He had the flu when he took the LSAT, he was on the waiting list but they overenrolled that year, blah blah blah.''

"You didn't like Henderson."

"He was a barrel of laughs. The Merle S. Coont scholar.''

"The what?"

"The top three students at Malhousie get a few bucks honorarium and get to be called the so-and-so scholar. Susan Green was the William Frazier Pilkington scholar. She was first in the class. Henderson was second.''

"And Greg Parker?"

"Only the top three get titles. Parker was farther down the ranks. Top six or seven percent, maybe.''

"So number three—does he move up to William Fretzer Pinkerton now that Green and Henderson are dead?''

I shrugged.

"Am I wrong? Doesn't number three become number one when you eliminate numbers one and two?''

"I guess that's right. I guess number three is number one now. I suppose he'll get the William Frazier Pilkington honorarium when we graduate.''

"This honorarium, are we talking big money?''

."A few hundred bucks, that's all. And the résumé value.''

"From a résumé point of view, the murders benefit numbers three through five. They all move two rungs up the ladder, am I right?''

I nodded.

"You know their names?"

"Number three's not on law review; he couldn't write worth a damn.'' I spelled out the name while Surgelato wrote it into a tiny leather notebook. "Number five's Jake Whittsen."

Surgelato lit a match and frowned at me over the flame. "Whittsen?"

"You probably interviewed him."

"He was at that party to clean up your office. With Parker and a bunch of you guys?"

"That's right."

He took a long drag of mentholated tobacco; smoke curled over his tongue like a white wave. "You skipped number four. Who's that?"

I smiled modestly.

Surgelato looked surprised. "You?"

"I'm smarter than I look."

A cop tapped at the door, came in, and handed Surgelato a few sheets of paper on a clipboard.

The lieutenant read them grimly, commenting, "Parker's wife made a positive ID. Wedding ring still on the bone, and they dug a belt buckle out of the waterlogged mess."

I closed my eyes for a minute. When I opened them, Surgelato was squatting beside my chair.

"Come on, I'll take you out for a bite."

"No."

"Coffee? A walk?"

I shook my head emphatically.

"Don't tell me it's the company."

I didn't tell him.

He eyed me sadly. "Cops are good guys, really. Ever hear the saying, 'If you don't like the police, next time you're in trouble, call a hippie'?"

"Sure, I read bumper stickers." I stood to leave, and he didn't stop me.

I stumbled out, trying not to think of Greg Parker as a "waterlogged mess."

When I got back to the office I found I'd missed a call from Silvio Bernstein. I went home and tried all night to reach him. I hung up on every reporter who phoned me, but I couldn't keep my line clear, so Silvio didn't get through.

The next morning, the *Chronicle* headline screamed at me from all the newsstands: "Law Student Washes Ashore." In smaller boldface, beneath a realistically unflattering picture of him, was the caption: "Did Gregory Parker Kill Classmates then Self?"

I went to the law review office and furiously dialed Surgelato's number. Parker's wife—his widow—didn't deserve that kind of innuendo from a fish wrap like the *Chronicle*.

But Lieutenant Surgelato, I was told, was not available for comment. I told the cop who I was, but all it got me was a cranky promise he'd tell Surgelato I'd phoned. Next time, goddam it, I *would* call a hippie.

Dean Sorenson sent a message to the law review office, requesting that I join him upstairs immediately. I sat there surrounded by pedestaled busts of John Marshall, Clarence Darrow, Alexander Hamilton, Charles Evans Hughes, and other renowned jurists, trying to shake the feeling they were going to ambush me. For half an hour, the dean sucked on his cheeks, solemnly elevated his brows, and laid out plans for yet another memorial service. He wondered whether the school should rent an organ.

When I got back downstairs, Gunnar Haas phoned to

offer his sympathy. I thought he might have ignored appearances for once and come down to see me.

Hatty McPherson had an attack of the screaming meemies when she found out about Greg. Unfortunately, she had it in the outer office. I dispatched some editors to track down her latest boyfriend, and we finally entrusted her to his loyal embrace. He seemed to find her histrionics adorable, and he informed me that this "murder thing" was difficult for Hatty because Greg Parker had mooned around after her and made himself a pest. I snapped that Hatty should be glad, then, and he recoiled as if a toad had hopped out of my mouth.

Harold Scharr, who now worked mornings, phoned from the U.S. Attorney's office and offered to come in and keep me company. I told him not to bother. Before he rang off, he asked if anyone had broken the news to Mary West.

I wasn't sure why Mary had taken it upon herself to plaster the neighborhood with Greg's picture, but it certainly indicated a particular interest in Greg's fate. Mary hadn't been to the office yet that morning, so I phoned her at home. I got no answer. I didn't think much of it, not realizing then that although we'd found Greg Parker, we'd lost Mary West.

Larry Tchielowicz came into the office, his thinning hair disheveled and his face flushed from his morning workout. He grabbed my elbow and frog-marched me into the inner office, away from a phalanx of editors asking questions about Greg that I couldn't possibly answer.

Tchielowicz was standing about six inches from me, and I was aware of the breadth of his chest and shoulders, aware that the face I'd once thought troll-like seemed extraordinarily strong and dear.

We "looked into each other's eyes," as the saying goes.

"Baby!" said a voice from the doorway. For a moment I ignored it, then I recognized it. I turned to see my parents, looking gaunt and sunburned.

I rushed to embrace the foolhardy pair.

I began to cry in Daddy's arms, noticing how skinny he was in his fuzzballed sweater. My mother, who'll cry over anything anyway, joined me. I kept saying, "You're all right!"

"Didn't Silvio tell you we were on our way home?" my father inquired placidly.

"You know politicians; they don't tell you anything till everyone's known it for a week."

I examined my mother carefully. She was thinner, but still pear-shaped in her polyester turtleneck and too-short bellbottoms. Her face had lost none of its Mrs. Santa Claus glow. "The cable said you were sick. What happened?"

"You should see what those poor people eat!"

"You didn't have to eat native, Mother!"

"There's no Howard Johnson's there, Baby."

"Why can't you just stay home like other people's parents?"

"Baby, if you saw what Reagan's policies have done to those poor, suffering people, you wouldn't ask." She began an impassioned tirade about how she couldn't stand by, *et cetera et cetera*, and it was every person's responsibility, *et cetera et cetera*, and what Jesus Christ and Mohandas Gandhi had had to say on the subject.

Daddy, a twinkle in his eye, ignored Mother and scrutinized Larry Tchielowicz. "Why don't you introduce us to this young man, Willa, before your mother breaks into 'The Battle Hymn of the Republic'!''

For this he earned a look of reproach from Mother, but she turned her attention to Larry and extended a hand, saying, ''June Jansson.''

My father followed suit. Larry, like everyone else who met my parents, seemed mildly surprised that my father's surname was Creel. My parents, ever in the vanguard, had chosen to give me my mother's name.

Larry introduced himself but made no move to go.

Daddy, faced with an immense hunk of male human who would not leave the room, displayed his characteristic wisdom and invited Larry to join us for lunch.

28

''PASS YOUR PLATE, Baby, and I'll put some of this on.''

''I don't want any of that.'' A dollop of greasy fish landed on my plate notwithstanding. Mother considered herself a vegetarian but viewed fish as wriggling vegetables.

She continued her saga. ''So the Honduran gestapo—

that's all they are!—and our own Nazi army advisors just plain booted us out. It makes me sick what That Man''— Reagan—''is doing, arming the power-drunk military! You should taste that fish; it's brain food. And you should see their troops! They're just children! An absolute disgrace. Eat it, Baby. You've gotten so skinny and pale!'' She turned to Larry. ''What kind of law are you going into? Tenants' rights? Environmental?''

''I'll be in the Judge Advocate General's Corps of the army.'' He looked straight at her, like a man breaking bad news. His upper lip curled.

Mother froze, fork halfway to her mouth. ''With what the army's doing in Central America, I wonder a smart young man like you wants to join.''

''I knew an army lawyer once,'' Daddy said thoughtfully.

''Do you prefer the army to be composed of uneducated, unemployable teenagers, then?'' Larry replied coolly.

Mother laid down her fork. ''I'd prefer to see it suffer a manpower shortage.''

''So that they reinstitute the draft?'' Larry went back to his lunch, a sauce-laden mess of soul food for which this restaurant, my parents' favorite, was famous.

Daddy continued his thought. ''I was stationed in Korea and I couldn't see one earthly reason boys should be dying there. I put down my gun, and they put me in the stockade.''

Larry regarded him with interest.

''I was put on trial in front of three officers, and a young boy your age was assigned to argue my case. He didn't do a bad job, all in all.''

"Huh!" Mother disagreed. "You spent two years in an army concentration camp!" She turned back to Larry. "How are you going to feel about putting nice young pacifists into prison?"

Daddy patted her hand. "The army lawyer was trying to keep me out of prison, not put me in."

"And what about the lawyer on the other side? This hired gun approach to justice is—"

"There isn't any other side," Larry interrupted, pushing away his plate. "The JAG Corps does legal defense. There's no prosecutor in a military court. I won't be putting anyone in jail!"

"And the other things the army does? Bombing children as they—"

"I'm sure he'll refrain from that, too, Mother."

"Lie down with dogs, wake up with fleas!" she insisted. "We were in this wonderful little village in Honduras, eating beans—they were a little like fava beans, I thought." She glanced at Daddy, and he nodded. "Well, all of a sudden—there were soldiers everywhere! And do you know who was leading them? U.S. Army! 'Advisors'!— Who do they think they're kidding! There they were, shooting off machine guns, rounding up villagers— even sick people, even a woman in labor! They stuff us all into trucks and scare us half to death. And do you know why?" She pointed an accusing finger at Larry. "*Training* maneuvers!"

Larry looked about as friendly as the dean's plaster busts, and I'd had as much of the topic as I could stand. "Did you hear about Susan Green, Mother?"

She stared at me, very red of face, her consciousness clearly back in Honduras.

"Remember Susan?" I persisted. "From my Standard orientation?"

"The girl who got so mad when I said I'd been raped?"

Larry choked on his beer, and I went on quickly. "She was killed, at the law school." I gave them a somewhat sanitized account of the three deaths.

Daddy rubbed his tow-colored hair, and I saw Larry glance from it to mine and stifle a smile. Daddy said, "And you've been stirring up the mud, I suppose?"

"Well, we did go talk to one of Susan's aunts about something we found out." I sketchily described the Koenig lawsuit.

Mother and Daddy exchanged glances.

"We knew the boy, Walter Bonomini," Daddy explained. "You remember that nice grocer on Columbus, the one who used to keep the gray mouser you loved so much?"

I nodded.

"That was his grandfather. He died not long after the trial, poor man. He was so proud of his grandchildren, introduced them to everyone when they came into the store. Walter was his pride and joy—accounting is considered a very exalted profession in Italy, you know, Willa. I remember reading that he'd lost his license and thinking how much that must have hurt his grandfather."

"So sad," Mother agreed. "Do you remember what a beauty the granddaughter was?" She turned to me. "That was Walter's sister. Melissa, I think her name was, an artist or a writer or something. I heard the whole family ended up moving to Alaska because of the publicity."

29

THE AIR BETWEEN Larry and me almost crackled. We returned our napkins to the table, Larry said something polite to my parents, and we left them staring after us in bewilderment.

"Melissa Whittsen's in Alaska right now. Mary West told me. She said Melissa went there to stay with her brother."

"Come on." Larry pulled me toward a pay phone. "Call Mrs. Koenig and find out if Susan ever met Bonomini's sister."

"Jake might have introduced them."

"In which case, Susan knew her as Melissa Whittsen, Jake's wife."

"But not Bonomini's sister? I get it." I made the call.

"Susan knew the Bonomini girl by sight," Mrs. Koenig confirmed, her voice tremulous. "The girl testified for that brother of hers, said how she was with him at a party when he met Mr. Pierce, the lawyer—or whatever he was—who stole our money. She said he'd have fooled anyone."

"So Susan was in the courtroom that day? She saw Melissa Bonomini testify?"

"Susan went with me to court every day. She was an angel."

I hung up. "Susan knew Melissa was Bonomini's sister, all right."

"Come on. Let's find Jake and see if Susan knew Melissa was his wife."

As we hurried back to Malhousie, I recounted (stopping frequently to gesticulate) Mary West's story about the photo of Melissa with her lover. "The lover has to be Clarence Day, Larry! Melissa was with him Christmas Eve!" It occurred to me that I'd been with Gunnar Haas Christmas Eve, but that was different. "Don't you see: Susan must have snapped that picture. She must have seen Melissa with Day and gotten suspicious about Day's ties to the Bonominis. Maybe she thought Day had screwed up her aunt's case on purpose—I mean, how often does a jury find in favor of an insured accountant over a white-haired old lady? That's why she was investigating Day's financial holdings!"

Larry kept his eyes averted and didn't comment.

One thing troubled me, though: "Even if Susan did know Melissa was Jake's wife, I can't imagine her showing him the picture." I halted again, but Tchielowicz marched on, forcing me to catch up. "She wouldn't have interfered in Jake's marriage that way—I mean, Susan could be cruel in a thoughtless, pompous kind of way, but I never knew her to be tacky." I waited for Tchielowicz to agree, but he remained silent. "Besides, Susan obviously didn't want people to know she was poking around in Day's affairs—look how she disguised that list of Day's property!''

I described Jake's reaction when I asked him about Melissa's infidelity. "He looked right at Greg Parker's chair. I'll bet Nosy found the picture in Susan's desk and showed it to Jake."

"What makes you think Parker knew Melissa Whittsen from a hot rock?"

"She was at the law review banquet with Jake last spring."

"Which means that last year's staff got to meet her. Most of this year's staff hadn't finished their articles yet. Most of us didn't write on till summer."

True. Not even Susan had finished her article in time to go to last year's banquet. I tried to visualize the banquet hall. I could see the usual professors, last year's editors, several of this year's. Hatty had been there, Harold, too. John Hancock Henderson, of course; he'd been the first of us to finish his article. But not Greg Parker.

"Maybe Greg found the picture in Susan's desk and showed it to someone else, someone who did know Melissa."

"Never say die."

"Susan and Greg are both dead, Larry. Maybe the middle man, the one who identified Melissa for Parker, is also dead. Maybe it was Henderson."

We'd reached the wide, shallow steps of Malhousie, and I turned to face Larry. "Maybe they all died because they'd seen that picture!"

Larry put his hands on my shoulders. "Willa, it's not important whether I agree or disagree. What's important is that you be careful, even with people you think you've ruled out!''

His words hit me like a bucket of water in the face: I was looking at a man who'd murdered someone with a baseball bat.

His eyes opened wide. "I didn't mean *me*!"

I heard a feeble voice at the top of the stair. "Hey lady!"

Lying in shadow like a discarded overcoat was Plead My Case.

"Friend of yours?" Larry inquired.

I trotted up to the old man, noticing fresh pigeon droppings on his fedora. "Were the cops rough on you the other day?"

He worked his lips over toothless gums, and I tried not to inhale the zoo smell of his clothing. With a significant nod of the head, he croaked, "Plead my case, lady?"

I slipped him a buck, saying, "Sure, call my secretary for an appointment."

I joined Tchielowicz at the door. "Goddam brownshirts roughed that old guy up—can you believe it?"

Speaking of the devil, I produced my ID.

"Well, if it wasn't one of us," Larry pointed at the basement stairs, "it was one of them." He inclined his head toward the patio.

"Does that old man look like public enemy number one to you?" I said it loudly enough for the two brownshirts to hear.

They smirked at one another, meticulously examining our IDs before letting us pass.

We looked for Jake Whittsen in the law review office, and we phoned his house, but we weren't able to track him down. Larry had a personal injury class with him later that afternoon, so we didn't bother looking around the school. Instead we went up to the cafeteria for some decent coffee.

The sound of clanging pinballs, jocular whoops, and clattering cutlery punctuated the roar of conversation in the overcrowded room. We bought some weak, scalding coffee and found a table near the door.

Harold Scharr came in, saw us, and dropped into a chair, lamenting Professor Miles' latest petty tyrannies.

Larry left to go to class, and I remained at the table, waiting for Harold to return with his lunch. He sat down, dubiously spearing what might have been an olive in an oozing portion of tamale pie. "Everything else was sold out. I'm not surprised this wasn't."

As he popped the olive into his mouth, I asked if he remembered Melissa Whittsen from the law review banquet.

"You're better looking," he assured me, frowning at a congealed yellow lump.

I was astonished at the form of his reply. Then I realized what had prompted it. "You've been listening to Mary, Harold. All gossip to the contrary, I'm not interested in Jake."

Looking uncomfortable, he made a show of pushing the lump to one side of his plate. "It's not just Mary. Even before, I thought—" He glanced at me. "You know."

So I'd worn my crush on my sleeve, for all the editors to see.

I noticed Harold looking over my left shoulder. I turned to find one of our articles editors standing there. Carla Sackett was a big, timid woman with brand new braces, of which she was painfully conscious.

"Willa! I'm glad I found you!" She flushed, taking care not to look at Harold; he was handsome enough to have that effect on shy women. "A woman called about Greg Parker."

"When? What did she say?" I had to shout over the "Aw right, aw right!" of the pinball players.

"Just now. She saw one of those posters, the ones Mary put on Market Street."

"Did she see Greg somewhere?"

Carla bent closer, so I could hear her. "She says she talked to him on the bus a week before Christmas. He asked her about the book she was reading. It was a library book, she'd just checked it out." She handed me a slip of paper. On it were a name, address, and phone number. "That's her."

A paper airplane landed on the table in front of me, then bounced off.

"She still has the book—it's way overdue. I asked her to look at the due date, and we figured out she must have checked it out the eighteenth." Carla blinked at me. "That's the day Greg—got lost."

"Did you ask her what time of day it was?"

Carla nodded. "Morning. She says Greg got off the bus at North Point. He told her he was going to choir practice."

Choir practice. "What bus were they on? Did she say?"

"Polk Street."

The Polk Street bus runs from the Civic Center to North Beach; a good bus to take from Malhousie to the Cathedral of Peter and Paul.

"Should I do something?" Carla Sackett tucked in her lips, hiding a faint gleam of metal.

Harold's hand slid across the plastic table. He plucked up the address. "We'll take care of it," he soothed her.

She cast a blushing glance at him, then nodded, rising. She took a few steps toward the door and was absorbed into the crowd.

Spots of color rose on Harold's thin cheeks as he read the slip of paper. "Poor bastard," he commented, folding his napkin and setting it beside his uneaten lunch.

"You're looking at the stupidest woman alive, Harold! Patricia Parker told me Greg missed choir practice, and I never till this minute connected it with Jane Day."

The color drained from Harold's face. "Are you all right, Willa?"

"Jane Day must have come to the law review office for Susan's picture that day. She must have found it in the filing cabinet with the manuscripts of Susan's article."

"What picture?" Another paper airplane skimmed our table top. Harold swatted it away.

"Here she is running for attorney general and Susan finds out about the affair and the breach of ethics with the property. Maybe something even bigger—throwing the case, or, who knows?" Nancy Drew couldn't be bothered with details. "The point is, how's it going to look if the state bar disciplines the aspiring attorney general's husband! Lady Jane has to keep Susan from telling, so she kills her. And she thinks she's safe till she finds out Susan's told Henderson all about it."

A chant grew up near the pinball machines: "Forty-five thou, forty-five thou; for forty-five thou we'll do anything, *anything*!"

I leaned forward, elbows on the table. "Henderson interviews at Day's law firm, see, and he mentions it—the property or the picture or whatever—to Lady Jane or Clarence. Maybe he thinks it'll force them to offer him a job. Instead, Lady Jane decides she has to get *him* out of the way, too.'' I paused for effect, but Harold was frowning at the chanters. "Anyway, so imagine how she feels when she runs into Parker before their choir practice and finds out *he's* seen the picture too!" I didn't know why Parker had mentioned the picture, but I was confident the reason would occur to me, by and by.

Harold shook his head. "Willa, you can't be serious! Jane Day is the soul of respectability and decorous conduct—she's our next attorney general, for Godsakes. And you're saying she's—" He looked over his shoulder, lowering his voice. "No, I won't republish the slander."

"She was at Malhousie the day Susan died, she came searching the office the week after, and she's got much more to lose than her husband if there's any kind of scandal about him!"

Harold put a finger to his lips to try to shush me. But I felt I'd burst if I didn't do something immediately.

I stood up. "Harold, wait till six o'clock, will you? Before you tell Lieutenant Surgelato about the lady on the bus?"

He stood, too, his chair bumping the one behind him. "Where are you going?"

"Just between us? You won't tell the lieutenant?"

He repeated, "Where are you going?"

"Lady Jane's house."

"What!"

His cry turned a few heads, and he was forced to smile weakly at curious onlookers. He came around to my side of the table, put his arm around me, and propelled me out to the lobby.

"Willa," he said grimly, "you're losing your grip. You can't go rambling this way to Jane Day. Promise me you won't!"

"Oh Harold! Didn't you see the morning paper?"

He nodded sourly. "I'm ashamed to admit I subscribe to that pile of—"

"They're saying Greg killed Susan and Henderson!"

He waited for some students to walk past us. "That's a whole separate issue. It's got nothing to do with—"

"Jane Day's going to get away with it!"

Harold turned away from me, took a few paces, then turned to face me again. "And what are *you* going to do? Go harass a confession out of her." He waved his arm. "For one thing, she's almost certainly innocent. And for another—have you ever seen her argue a case? Attila the Hun couldn't scare that confident little smile off her face!"

"Don't worry, I'm not going to confront her! I just want to know if she went to choir practice the morning Greg disappeared."

"Let the police ask her."

"If *they* ask her, she'll know something's up."

"Besides which, her ladyship's probably still at the office!"

"I might not get in to see her if I go there—she has too much control over her work environment. Besides, why would I go to her office? What's my pretext? If I go to her house, I can 'accidently' run into her on the street when she gets out of her car."

Harold's jaw dropped and he shook his head. "That's completely transparent!"

I smiled, taking a few steps backward, toward the door. "She'll be too polite to say so."

Harold extended a long, Bill Blassed arm. "Wait a minute! Nice aristocratic ladies who live in Pacific Heights do not—Willa!"

But I was already running out the door.

30

HALF OF SAN Francisco knew where Jane and Clarence Day lived. The house had been written up in *Architectural Digest*, and the Days occasionally allowed charitable organizations to conduct tours of the quasi-gothic castle.

Bus connections were as complicated as a treasure map, though; the wealthy don't have to worry about convenience of transit. I wasted an hour at various bus stops, nervously watching the sky. The wind had died to a whisper, and ragged black clouds were tumbling over the horizon. In San Francisco, lack of wind means one of two things: in summer, it means fog; any other time, it means rain. Once again, I mourned the loss of my Scotchguarded tweed jacket, resenting poor John Henderson for having turned it into "evidence."

By the time I reached the Day mansion, a leaden canopy of clouds darkened the afternoon, adding romance to the massive stone house, with its beveled windows and green copper fittings. A young boy in pleated khaki pants and a shoulder-padded shirt glanced at the sky uncertainly and continued polishing the baby-blue Rolls Royce in the semi-circular driveway.

His presence made it impolitic for me to position myself in front of the house. I went around the corner, to the side of the mansion, and found myself looking down a dizzyingly steep hill. Beyond the miniature castles and plantation houses of Pacific Heights, the marina bobbed with tiny sailboats and the graphite bay flickered with whitecaps. To my left, the Golden Gate Bridge stretched to the hazy hills of Marin, its peaked towers lost in clouds.

I thought of my own front window panorama of treeless street, shared-wall apartment buildings, and crisscrossed streetcar wires. I guess Pacific Heights is the neighborhood Tony Bennett left his heart in.

Beside me, a ten-foot, ornately spiked iron fence rose out of the concrete, running a full block downhill, until it met a stone wall. On the other side of the fence, a square-topped rhododendron hedge hid the house from view. I tried to peer through the hedge but saw only its broad, shiny leaves.

I couldn't resist: I got a toehold on the metal grape-leaves of the fence and hoisted myself high enough to peek over the glossy hedge top. A sloping emerald lawn, surrounded by rhododendron-bordered walks, lay below.

I was just noticing a patio when I slipped part way back down the fence, skinning my hand and tearing my jeans. I was about to beat a dispirited retreat when I heard Lady

Jane's voice. I slipped again, losing a small chunk of forehead to a metal grapeleaf. I landed on both knees and one hand, swearing.

Lady Jane stood in a gap of the hedge, watching me. "I saw you from an upstairs window," she told me pleasantly.

"Oh." I picked myself up, brushing off my knees and hands.

"There's a gate here. Do come in." A vote is a vote, I guess.

I entered in the conventional manner, noticing an inch of exposed leg where the fence had bitten my jeans. But overall, I was pleased with myself: I'd achieved my object. Jane Day was granting me an audience.

She led me to an alabaster patio equipped with a wet bar. She motioned me to sit at a malachite table and she poured two sherries from a decanter. Her hand was steady and her face composed. She couldn't have been more nonchalant if she'd expected me.

"Nice yard," I offered. Sitting with her in the cool tranquility of her garden, it was difficult to imagine her smashing in a couple of skulls.

A voice called out from the house. "Jane?"

"Out here, Day."

Clarence Day stepped through beveled French doors onto the patio. He was neatly attired in silver wool that matched his hair. "That West girl!" he said before he saw me. "She's driving me—"

Jane Day said, "You remember the editor-in-chief of Malhousie's law review, don't you?"

He was clearly disconcerted, but that was nothing compared to how I felt. I didn't know what Mary West was up to, but I was beginning to feel like the spiders' dinner.

"She was climbing the fence," Jane continued serenely.

Day frowned. A few lines creased his forehead, but otherwise he looked quite young, a weathered forty instead of a well-preserved sixty. He appeared to be waiting for an explanation.

Too bad, because I didn't have one. I sipped my sherry and smiled vacuously.

A personal injury lawyer to the core, he glanced at my gouged forehead and inquired, "You're not badly hurt, Miss uh—?"

"Jansson. No, I'm fine."

He went to the bar and poured himself two fingers of whiskey. He didn't sit with us. He remained at the bar, looking out over his sea of manicured grass.

"Any progress on the homicide investigations? I was sorry to read about—Parker, is it?" Jane Day smoothed a nonexistent wrinkle from her cashmere knit skirt.

I swirled the sherry in my glass. I hate sherry. "You knew Greg Parker. At least, he knew you. He said you sang together in the Christmas choir at Peter and Paul's— or you would have, if he'd lived long enough."

"Really? You know, I thought the picture in the paper looked familiar, but then we've interviewed so many of your editors. . . ."

"You probably saw him at some of the choir practices."

Something flashed in her lapis-blue eyes.

"In fact, Greg went to choir practice the day he disappeared, the eighteenth of December. Maybe you saw him at the cathedral."

She smiled her little smile; Harold was right—Attila the Hun couldn't rattle her. "Possibly. I doubt I'd have recognized him."

"But you were there that day?" I tried to sound like I was just making conversation.

"I made it to most of the practices, I think. It's pleasant to do something unrelated to law now and again, don't you find?"

With eight articles to edit, four classes to get through, spring finals to take, a nine-week bar review course and the bar exam staring me in the face, I could only suppose so. I swirled my sherry and nodded.

I tried one last gambit. "They've made quite a bit of progress on the murders, actually. They found a photograph that shows a motive for at least one, and maybe all of them."

That got Clarence Day's attention. "A photograph? Of what?"

I shook my head coyly. "They haven't come right out and told me. But I have my suspicions."

Jane Day fondly regarded the pearl on her finger. "Well, whatever his motives, and in spite of his crimes, it's a shame your Mr. Parker came to such a sad end."

"Greg Parker didn't kill anyone!"

Lady Jane glanced at Clarence. "Of course," she soothed. "We can hardly make assumptions at this point." She stood. "Dinner at seven, Day. Come along, Ms.—"

"Jansson."

"I'm on my way to Malhousie, as it happens." She looked up at the rain clouds. "Can I offer you a lift?"

We walked together through the poshly outfitted house (white silk walls, Hepplewhite chairs, and half the world supply of malachite). She left me standing in the portal while she consulted with the well-dressed car waxer. After a few minutes, he handed her the keys and she motioned for me to join them.

I climbed into the front seat of the Rolls, and Jane Day slid behind the wheel, saying, "I love to drive, don't you, Ms. Jensen?"

"Jansson. No, I hate it."

I heard the back door slam and turned to see the young man, a milk-skinned blond, ensconced behind me. We exchanged strained smiles.

By the time we reached Malhousie, rain was battering the car and steaming up the windows. I sank deeper into the cream leather seat, instinctively suspicious of the young stranger behind me.

Jane Day stopped at the entrance of Malhousie's garage. The brownshirt with the Adam's apple appeared at her window. He was draped in green vinyl and carried a clipboard in a plastic bag. It was the first time I'd noticed a guard posted there.

Lady Jane pressed a button and her window slid silently open, just a crack. She drew back as rain spattered her hardwood dash. "Jane Day," she informed him. "To see Professor Haas."

I tried not to register surprise. After all, there could be a dozen reasons why she'd want to confer with Gunnar Haas. They might be on some bar committee together. He might have asked her to conduct a guest lecture.

The guard checked his clipboard, wiping rain from its plastic cover. "Go on in, Mrs. Day. Professor said to expect you." He straightened up; all we could see of him was dripping vinyl.

Lady Jane tapped the window to reclaim his attention. "Would you mind unlocking the basement door so we don't have to go around front and get wet?"

The guard squatted beside the window, blinking rainwater out of his eyes. "Sorry, Mrs. Day. They've put a slip-bolt on the inside so's it won't open with a key anymore."

That was news to me. A sign that the police believed the murderer had a key? Well, apparently she didn't. And apparently she knew the door required one, though she'd once claimed not to know the door even existed.

"Then I'm sorry to trouble you, but do you suppose you could go around yourself and let us in? I'm not dressed for rain, as you can see."

I tried to catch the brownshirt's eye. I didn't want to be alone in the basement with Jane Day and her young henchman. I volunteered to go myself, but no one listened to me. The weasel-faced guard disappeared into the downpour, and Jane Day drove down the ramp into the cavernous garage. She parked beside Gunnar's Alfa Romeo.

I got out quickly and walked to the basement door. I knocked and rattled the knob. Glancing behind me, I saw Jane Day nod to her passenger. He went around to the trunk, and I realized then what Lady Jane's weapon had been. A jack. A simple tire iron. Something you can take out of your trunk, use quickly, and slip back into place to be cleaned later.

I rattled the knob again, then began hammering on the door. The day Susan Green was killed, Jane Day had given a speech at the law school. Maybe she'd gone out to her car, leaving the basement door ajar. Maybe she'd taken a tire iron from her trunk, waited till no one was around, and reentered through the basement door. Maybe she'd tiptoed into the law review office, found Susan working at her desk, and smashed her skull. Maybe she'd done the same when Henderson was murdered. Maybe she'd do it again today.

The rain continued beating down, making the dim underground chamber fiercely damp and cold. Jane Day approached, her chignoned head in shadow. Over her shoulder she called, "You know what I need, Pierce!"

Pierce! That's what Mrs. Koenig had called the "lawyer" who'd defrauded her. Maybe they didn't mean to wait, maybe Pierce already had the tire iron in his hand! I pounded the door frantically, almost scared enough to kick the damned thing in.

Luckily, I didn't have to. At that moment, it opened from the inside, and I fell into Jake Whittsen's arms.

31

THERE WAS A moment of stunning anti-climax as young Pierce pulled Jane Day's briefcase out of the trunk and walked toward us. Jane Day thanked Jake for opening the door, and she and Pierce walked off down the hall together. They greeted the brownshirt on the stair, and the three of them Dopplered away, discussing the weather.

I rested my forehead against Jake's chest, waiting for my heart to stop hammering.

"What's the matter?" Jake cupped my chin in his hand and tilted my face up. "You're all scratched up."

"I've been doing a little climbing. God, am I glad to see you! I don't suppose there's any coffee in the office?"

"I just made a pot."

The coffee tasted like paint thinner, but I didn't care. I guzzled most of an unwashed mugful. "Did Tchielowicz talk to you in personal injury?"

"No, I skipped class. What's up?" He leaned against the mailboxes.

"I wanted to ask you something about Melissa."

His facial muscles tensed. He'd had quite enough of discussing Melissa with Mary West, no doubt.

"I don't want to pry, but, well, it has to do with the murders, I think."

He shook his head skeptically.

"Jake, I know Melissa is Walter Bonomini's sister."

"Yeah. That's right." He sounded only mildly surprised. "Do you know Walter?"

"No, but Susan Green did. It was Susan's aunt who sued him."

"Is that right?" He covered his eyes with his hand, dragging it slowly down over his face. "Poor Wally. He messed up once, trusted some bozo, and that was the end of his career. He's gone six, eight weeks at a time now, fishing the Gulf. You know how cold it gets out there?"

I motioned for him to follow me into the inner office. Unfortunately, Hatty McPherson was sitting at her desk editing a manuscript and sipping a Tab. Her head jerked up at the sound of the door opening. Her hand went to her throat, making her look like the generic pretty-girl-about-to-get-murdered of theater marquees.

"Hatty, do you mind if I talk to Jake alone for a few minutes?"

"Why?"

"We're solving the murders," I joked.

As usual, Hatty did not look amused. "I'll get soaked if I go home now."

"You could go upstairs and grab a bite."

Hatty looked horrified by the very idea of eating. Nevertheless, she slipped on her wooden-soled high heels and clomped away, taking the manuscript with her.

Jake eyed me mistrustfully. "What was that supposed to mean—'solving the murders'?"

"Jake, when we were talking about Melissa the other day, you looked over there at the chair Greg Parker used to sit in."

He glanced at the chair again, his body stiffening. "Did I?"

"And then Mary told me someone showed you a picture of Melissa at a party—"

"Mary! Christ!" He kicked Hatty's bottom drawer shut.

"I'm sorry to bring it up, but the picture could be critically important—"

"Bullshit! What are you *really* after? What are you driving at?"

I stepped between him and the door. "I think I know who showed you the picture. Greg found it in Susan's desk and brought it to you, didn't he? He told you Melissa was cheating—"

"No one told me!"

"You already knew? Even before you saw the picture?"

"Get out of my way!" His face suffused with color, a vein throbbed in his forehead.

"Please! Just tell me who was in the picture."

"You want to know about the picture?" His hands curled into fists. "Why don't you ask Tchielowicz?"

"Tchielowicz?"

"He didn't like us going out together, did he?"

"*Larry* showed you the picture?"

His eyes opened wider, his nostrils flared. And he looked at Greg Parker's chair.

Then he pushed me aside, slamming the flimsy door behind him.

Why don't you ask Tchielowicz?

I thought of Larry's reticence about his juvenile record, thought about Conrad Hall, who'd had it coming, thought about Henderson's phone call to the orphanage, thought about Parker's anonymous warning, "Investigate Larry Tchielowicz."

And I remembered Larry's own words: *Don't trust anyone, even someone you think you've ruled out.*

32

TEN MINUTES LATER, Tchielowicz burst into the office. "Here you are! Are you *crazy*—climbing Day's fence?"

He crossed to my desk in a few bounds and put his big hands on my shoulders. I think he meant to embrace me, but I pulled away.

"Are you all right, Willa? I went after you as soon as Harold told me where you—"

"*What?* You *didn't* go to—"

"Clarence Day said you tried to hop his fence—very athletic of you!"

"You talked to Clarence Day?" I considered slugging him. "My visit was supposed to be accidental! Casual! What do you suppose he thought when a big hulking jock came looking for me?"

"Casual! You tried to climb his damned fence! Or were you going to 'drop in'?"

"I didn't climb the fence! I peeked over it! And anyway, I got in to see Lady Jane, didn't I?"

"Yes? And?"

"And I asked her—very nonchalantly—if she'd gone to

choir practice the day Parker disappeared. Harold told you about the woman who saw Greg on the bus?''

"Yeah. So? Was Jane Day at choir practice?''

I was forced to admit, "She didn't really say.''

"And that was completely predictable! Jane Day's too smart to tell you anything she doesn't want you to know—even if she is a murderess, which I don't believe for a minute!''

"Jane Day's too smart? And what am I—a dumb blonde?''

Tchielowicz turned away, I think to hide a smile. "Whittsen wasn't in class, by the way.''

"He was just here.'' I sorted noisily through some galley proofs. "I asked him about the picture.''

Tchielowicz frowned, began to speak, then closed his mouth again.

I pushed aside the proofs, asking snidely, "Don't you want to know what Jake said?''

"What did he say?''

I considered telling him, but an inner voice advised caution. "He said it was none of my business. He wouldn't talk about it.''

Larry dropped into Greg Parker's chair, rubbing his nose pensively. "What about the connection between Melissa and Susan's aunt?''

"He seemed surprised by it.''

"You didn't push it, did you? You didn't turn it into a confrontation?''

"What's that supposed to mean?''

"You've been going around confronting everybody with what you think you know—''

"No I haven't!'' I nearly mentioned Jake's pronouncement and Parker's warning, just to prove I'd been keeping my mouth shut. But I recognized the logical flaw in speaking up to prove my reticence.

"Sometimes I think it's a miracle no one's done you in yet! Either that or you've been wrong about everything so far." Tchielowicz inclined his head. "You're sure Whittsen didn't say anything about the picture?"

"I told you: he said it was none of my business."

I gathered up the galleys of my own article (about political sanctuary for illegal aliens) and tossed Tchielowicz the galleys of his (about taxing wholly-owned subsidiaries—a real snoozer, in my opinion). They were slated to appear in our spring issue and needed proofreading.

He tucked the galleys under his sweater. "Want a ride home? It's wet out there."

I thought of my tweed jacket, warming baggies of contraband in some police locker, and I accepted the offer.

Five minutes later, I was shivering under the black eaves of the patio, waiting for Larry to pull up his car. In the recess of a casement window above me, a chorus of pigeons cooed and tapped. I hoped Plead My Case had found shelter like the rest of the native fauna.

I got soaked dashing down the steps and into Larry's double-parked Chevy. He handed me some paper towels and I dried my face, then noticed a trickle of water running down his temple. All I did was touch the towel to his face; maybe it was the intimacy of the gesture, maybe the coziness of the steamy, overheated car.

I dropped the towel, flustered.

Larry pulled away from Malhousie, smiling. I picked up the paper and wiped a circle of condensation from the passenger window. A pair of women dashed past, daintily jumping puddles in their high heels, their briefcases held aloft like umbrellas.

I sneaked a glance at Larry. His face was red with cold, and his hair looked thinner than ever, dripping wet. Moreover, he was argumentative, conservative, conventional, even paternalistic. I couldn't believe I'd let this feeling sneak up on me.

"Can you take me to my parents' flat?"

"Sure."

I told him how to find the place, and when we got there, politeness compelled me to invite him in. To my surprise, he accepted.

Daddy answered the door, wearing the chef's apron that had been my belated Christmas present to him. He pulled us through the hall and into the kitchen, showing off the mouth-searing Szechwan meal he was methodically preparing. He insisted Larry stay to sample it. "I can make tofu taste like chicken and pork in the same dish—you'll see."

The smell of garlic, sesame oil, and ginger extended to the living room, where we found Mother sitting cross-legged on an Indian cushion, open books spread out around her. She was looking for Great Quotations with which to season yet another letter to the President. This evening's missive, we found, concerned a so-called Victims' Rights Bill. Mother called this particular hobbyhorse "a blueprint for the inhumane treatment of prisoners," and she rode it often.

"They treat them like animals, and when they try to resist, when they try to hang on to a bit of dignity, the lawless prison system uses it as an excuse for more institutionalized violence!'' She scooted a dish of mints across the floor toward Larry. ''No artificial colors!''

I noticed with dismay that there was a film projector and a big can of film on the coffee table. Mother was forever checking documentaries out of the library. Our dinner guests were frequently subjected to conversation stoppers like *The Rise and Fall of the Third Reich* and *Harvest of Shame* with their coffee. Tonight's scratchy polemic was bound to be about prison reform, the last thing in the world I wanted to watch with Larry Tchielowicz.

When my mother began soliciting Larry's views on victims' rights, I escaped into the kitchen to help Daddy. I heard Mother cry, ''You can't believe that!'' and supposed Larry's opinion was significantly less sentimental than hers.

Mother has a high, carrying voice, and Larry a low, quiet one, so Daddy and I heard all of her points but none of Larry's. Apparently he rebutted her stock arguments; she chose instead to draw on personal anecdotes about forgiveness of those who do one harm.

I left Daddy in the kitchen and began setting out the bowls and the chopsticks. From the dining room, I could see Mother's earnest face as she looked up at Larry. He was seated on the canvas couch, his back to me, being his usual, irritatingly dispassionate self, arguing justice to someone who believed in mercy.

Mother was insisting, ''You have to forgive, no matter how grievous, how permanent the injury against you, or it burns a hole in your heart!'' She tapped her chest to indicate the location of her own bleeding organ.

I set down the dishes with something of a clatter, wishing Mother would stop. Larry heard me and turned, smiling.

Mother, catching sight of me, used me as an example. "Like Willa! When that boy from Boston gave Willa the herpes, she tore herself apart hating him!"

Larry blanched. His eyes grew round and his jaw slackened. He looked like he'd just taken a slap in the face. Then he turned back to Mother.

She continued. "It wasn't till Willa let go of her anger that she was able to get on with her life!"

At dinner, I sat across the table from Larry, but I couldn't look him in the eye. I poked at my food and entertained a lot of bitter thoughts about my life.

Larry opted to stay for the movie, in spite of Mother's cheerful announcement that it dealt with "the barbarism and despair of prison life."

I sat in the dark watching Larry's profile as the film took us on a relentlessly bleak prison tour. He showed little expression until the documentary concluded with the words of a much younger Julian Warneke: "We can continue to brutalize, deprive, and objectify them—but we do have to release them eventually. And the question is: Will they recover, or will they reciprocate?"

For a moment I thought Larry was going to smile, but then he frowned, glancing at me.

When Daddy turned the lights back on, Larry got up immediately and said good night. He forgot to offer me a ride home, so I spent the night in my old room staring at my psychedelic posters and thinking: So much for the budding romance of Larry Tchielowicz and Willa Jansson.

I went to the office early the next morning. I found the door unlocked and coffee already made. I poured myself a cup and started into the inner office. The door was closed and the lights were still off. I opened the door, clicked on the light, and stepped inside.

Something hit me from behind like a wrecking ball.

33

THERE WAS A voice in my head. It said, "Shit, you're dead."

Then there was a second voice. "Not till you find out who did it."

I thrashed onto my back. That probably saved my life. Apparently my attacker found it difficult to strike my face. Too personal, I guess, or too gory. All I know is that I flopped over like a fish and nothing else happened.

I mean nothing. I willed my eyes to open. They would not. I willed my limbs to move and could almost hear them reply, "Fat chance." When I was a child, my parents took me swimming in the ocean in Mexico. The waves dragged me under and mopped the rocky sea bottom with my face. I had a vague impression I was back there. There was a roaring in my ears, and I was dragged out of consciousness.

I oozed back into being, and saw Larry Tchielowicz hovering over me.

Dear God! Not Larry!

I tried to squirm away, but the pain was blinding.

His big hands pinned my shoulders. "Whoa!" he ordered. "Keep still till the ambulance gets here!"

"Ambulance!" I could hear the relief in my voice. He'd called an ambulance; that meant he'd found me, not attacked me.

I kept my eyes tightly closed; fluorescent light stabbed through the lids. "See," I gloated weakly, "I have not been wrong about everything so far."

He brushed the hair off my face. "Consider yourself vindicated."

I heard Harold Scharr's frightened voice. "I've got the blankets. God, I wish they'd get here!"

I could smell mothballs as one of them spread a blanket over me. I tried to push it off, nauseated by the odor. The movement sent spasms of pain through my temples to the roots of my hair. I left the blanket on.

When the pain subsided to a throb, I informed Tchielowicz, "Harold thinks I'm better looking than Melissa Whittsen." I'm not sure why I found this relevant, but I did.

Larry touched his lips to mine, murmuring, "You are."

I basked in the compliment. Then I opened my eyes to a squint. "You said you weren't at the law review banquet."

His big face went in and out of focus. "What? Oh, I see." His tone changed to ironic amusement. "That doesn't mean I haven't met her since, Nancy Drew."

I could make out Harold Scharr and Alfonsin the janitor

squatting behind Larry. I closed my eyes, spacing out on the smell of naphthalene.

After a while an ambulance came and took me away.

It was just a concussion and some broken skin. I won't bore you with an account of my first day in the hospital. I was so medicated and out of touch that I was able to watch daytime TV without cringing.

I was also able to tell Lieutenant Surgelato everything I knew about the incident.

"I walked in the door and something hit me."

"What else?" The lieutenant's mega-brows bristled as he tapped the railing of my bed.

"I rolled over. Then I woke up."

I was flat on my back. Last time I'd looked straight up at a cop that way, he'd been about to grab my ankles and help his partner carry me to a fenced "temporary detention compound."

At least Surgelato skipped the usual flirtation; I guess my gauze turban wasn't very attractive. He stalked out of the room, two homicide inspectors in his wake.

By the following morning, I was fit company for visitors. And I had plenty of them over the next four days. Harold sneaked me in a joint, which we smoked together while the lady in the next bed snored. Larry came every day, and so did my parents, of course. Gunnar Haas sent flowers, but so did half the faculty; he didn't visit me.

Hatty McPherson arrived with some of the other editors. She greeted me by blurting out that no one had seen Mary West since Monday—the day Parker's body had turned up. Hatty, looking even more frightened and skeletal than usual, tearfully informed me that she was resigning and there was nothing I could do about it. Larry shooed her away, and came back wishing it were still customary to slap hysterical women.

"Anything else I should know?"

He shifted his bulk from one topsidered foot to another. "Your apartment. I went there with your parents the other day to get your stuff." He glanced at the sweatclothes I prefer to pajamas. "I think your place was ransacked."

I tried to sit up. "Ouch."

"A couple of your drawers were open, there was stuff all over the floor. And I think someone might have spent the night in your bed."

"And ate my porridge, too, I suppose."

"Porridge? It looked to me like you live on coffee and sugarless gum, baby bear."

I realized I hadn't once thought about tobacco since I'd been smashed on the head. The minute I had this happy relevation, I wanted a cigarette more than anything else in the universe. "What did my parents say?"

"They didn't say anything." He seemed troubled. "I didn't want to upset them, so I didn't mention it either."

And I decided not to mention that my apartment always looks ransacked.

34

MY HOSPITAL BILL was approaching the national debt, and my mother was due to bring me more of her awful soup. I browbeat the doctor into signing my release form (they should be required to read you your rights before they take your clothes away) and I phoned a cab. I probably should have waited a couple of hours till my parents were up and around, or till Larry's morning class was over, but I was impatient.

I decided to stop by the office. With Henderson and Parker dead, and Hatty overwrought, the technical staff had been decimated. Galleys of our spring issue would be piling up, unproofed. I thought I'd better pick them up and do them myself, at home. I'd worry about my classes some other week; if I ended up in the top three of my graduating class, Don Surgelato would probably arrest me.

I told the cab driver where to go and he said, "That's the place they're having all them murders, right? It's gotta be one of them editors, the way I look at it." He twisted his head around so that his eyes remained on the road while he more or less faced me.

"Why do you say that?"

"Because they're the ones that's always there, you know, so they can see when someone's alone. Anyone else, he'd have to hang around there too much, waiting for an opportunity. Somebody'd be bound to notice 'em." He nodded. "Besides, you can't tell me the weapon ain't hid in that office somewheres. It's gotta be. You can't go walking around no hallways with a pipe or a hammer or whatever and no one notice."

I found the office unlocked and the coffee made, but this time I took a good look around before I stepped inside.

I poured myself a cup of coffee; it tasted like it had been brewed before I'd gone to the hospital. Then I sat at my desk, which was piled high with galleys. Aside from the smell of printer's ink, there was nothing to indicate that I was in a law review office. The desks were bare of manuscripts, the law reporters were neatly tucked into the bookcase, all traces of legal memorabilia—from flow-charts of federal agencies to squeeze-toy gavels—had vanished. There were no notebooks, no casebooks, no prefab outlines, no hornbooks, no "law in a nutshell" paperbacks on any of the desks. Even small personal items like coffee mugs, lunch bags, calendars, and favorite pens were gone. A layer of dust covered Susan's and Henderson's desks.

I began to think about the cab driver's theory. It was true that anyone other than an editor, or possibly someone on the faculty, would have been conspicuous around the office. Anyone in the outer office could have looked through the acrylic partition and seen Susan, then Henderson, sitting alone. But it seemed to me that only another editor, someone familiar with our routines and schedules, would have felt confident of remaining alone with the victim long enough to commit murder.

And that would seem to rule out my pet suspect, Jane Day.

I tried to separate my suspicions from her actual behavior and decided that a benign interpretation was possible for all but one of her actions. She'd searched the filing cabinet.

When I'd walked in on her the week after Susan's murder, Jane Day had been about to remove the drafts of Susan Green's article; that's how it had seemed to me at the time.

She'd claimed she was looking for the draft of her own student article, and it was possible that she'd been telling me the literal truth; lawyers will do that sometimes, if it doesn't prejudice their chances of getting what they want. But Lady Jane must have realized no one would keep a draft of a published article for fifteen years.

No one except the author. I still had drafts of the *Stanford Daily* articles that had almost gotten me kicked out of school; they seemed more real to me than the published versions, somehow.

Maybe Lady Jane had been equally sentimental about her own draft; maybe she'd misplaced it, maybe she really had been searching for it in our filing cabinet.

But why would she expect to find it with Susan Green's manuscripts?

I phoned the Hall of Justice (now there's a euphemism!) and asked for Lieutenant Surgelato. For once, they put me through to him.

"Where are you?" he demanded.

"At the law review office."

"Alone?"

"Well, yes."

He swore, briefly but colorfully. "I'll get a man there—"

"No, no, I'm leaving right now. Even as we speak. I just have a quick question. About Jane Day's article."

"What about it? I told you—" He stopped, repeating, "What about it?"

So he *did* have it! Lady Jane had searched for it after Susan's murder, but the police had already taken it away. "When does it come out of the evidence locker?"

"When it stops being evidence. Now what's this about?" His tone grew suspicious. "*Really* about?"

I could think of only one reason why the police would want to take the manuscript into evidence. "It's odd that Susan was reading it when she died."

"Is it?"

"I mean, the published version was right beside her on the bookcase."

He didn't respond.

"And it's an old article; there wouldn't have been any editorial reason for Susan to read it."

"That right? You ever talk to her about it?"

"No."

"What's this about, Ms. Jansson? What are you fishing for?"

"It's just that some of the editors thought, they wanted to know how things are—" My head ached; I was finding prevarication difficult. "With all this trouble, with our reputation—"

"You people and your damned reputations!" he exploded.

For the first time, I considered what it might be like for Surgelato, questioning people like Dean Sorenson and Professor Miles and Jane Day. They barely tolerated *me*, and (as someone at the dean's party had observed) I was "quasi-professorial."

"We *are* a disgusting group!" I agreed.

"I didn't say that." His tone was cautious.

"Well, thanks for—"

"And you didn't say what this is really about."

"Just a status check."

I listened to him breathe—he seemed to breathe more heavily when he was thinking. It reminded me of a line my father used to read me, about Winnie-the-Pooh being a bear of very little brain, so that when he thought, he thought as thoughtfully as he could.

I hung up before Surgelato could think of anything more to ask me.

I was pleased with myself. I'd figured out, and confirmed, that Susan Green had been reading a draft of Jane Day's article at the moment of her death. Maybe I needed a good bop on the head now and then to keep the machinery humming.

On the other hand, every part of my head hurt: my eyeballs throbbed, my scalp was tender, even my teeth ached. And solving the minor mystery of Jane Day's article didn't get me very far.

I glanced at Henderson's desk and remembered watching Gunnar Haas search it. If he hadn't been looking for his article on the Swedish statute, then what had he been looking for? How had page six of the opus found its way downstairs?

My mind drifted to Gunnar's uncharacteristic championing of Henderson's petty battle to rise to the top of our masthead, and I began to see a connection.

Suppose Gunnar Haas had given Susan his article on the Swedish statute, leaving the office moments before she was murdered. Suppose John Henderson had come along later and found Susan's body. He'd have spotted Gunnar Haas' article on her desk. Henderson had kept track of our manuscripts; he'd have known it was a new arrival. The absence of a cover letter would have told him it had been personally delivered. He'd have realized Gunnar Haas had recently left the murder scene.

Maybe John Hancock Henderson had taken Gunnar's manuscript off Susan's desk, hoping to put the law review's faculty advisor in his debt. He must have known he'd never succeed Susan as editor-in-chief without help from the faculty. And if he wanted that Wall Street job, he urgently needed to strengthen his résumé.

And Gunnar Haas would certainly have preferred a little polite blackmail to becoming a murder suspect. Admitting he'd been alone with Susan shortly before her murder wouldn't have done his tenure bid any good—especially if the murders remained unsolved.

He must have been looking for page six of his manuscript when he searched Henderson's desk that day. Maybe he'd feared Henderson intended further blackmail. Maybe he'd been right.

If John Henderson could look at Susan Green's dead body and see an opportunity for advancement, there was no telling what he might demand of Gunnar besides the

convocation of a faculty meeting. If Gunnar Haas had
ended up killing John Henderson, I could hardly blame
him.

But I couldn't imagine Gunnar killing Susan. Or Greg.

My eyes strayed to Greg Parker's chair—I could almost
see him sitting there, slumped and cross-legged, like a
plump dowager. I couldn't imagine Greg killing Susan,
either. Surgelato's double-murder-followed-by-suicide theory was wishful thinking.

Still looking at the chair, I remembered the cab driver's
theory that the murderer had to be one of us. I remembered what he'd said about the weapon being hidden
downstairs, about it being impossible to walk around the
halls with a pipe or a—

A pipe. I looked up from Greg's chair to the ceiling, a
low-hung tangle of pipes.

When Jake Whittsen had glanced at that chair, I'd assumed he'd been thinking of Greg Parker. But maybe not.

I walked over to the chair and stood on it. From that
vantage point, I could peer into the intimidating maze of
metal. I reached my hand up and traced several pipes till
they continued out of arm's reach. Flakes of rust and des-
iccated fly parts fell over my face and arm; I nearly sneezed
myself off balance.

And then my fingers found it: a piece of pipe that went
nowhere. It was wedged in between several other pipes
like part of the plumbing. A few jerks and it dislodged.

It was a two-foot black metal tube, caked at one end
with a lighter substance I realized was probably blood,
some of it my own.

A voice from the doorway inquired, "What have you
got there, Willa?"

I turned to see Jake Whittsen leaning against the door-frame, handsome as ever with his coffee-colored eyes and his inscrutably noble face.

35

JAKE STARTED TOWARD me, scowling.

I looked down at him and thought, this is Walter Bonomini's brother-in-law, and Walter Bonomini helped *somebody* rob Susan's aunt. I squeaked, "*You're* Pierce, aren't you?"

He reached out for the pipe, but I brandished it, Greg's chair wobbling beneath me. "I'll fight you!"

He smiled. Such was the terror my threat inspired.

I'm not sure whether Jake yanked the chair out from under me or I toppled off of my own accord, but it went sailing across the room on its casters. I found myself on the floor staring up at six feet of murderous male. I tried to roll over onto the pipe, but Jake easily wrenched it out from under me.

I focused on the hand that held the pipe. Jake's knuckles were white, and cords of muscle stood out on his forearm.

I wrapped both hands around the still-lowered end of

the pipe and yanked it, almost managing to tug Jake off balance. When he pulled the pipe up, he pulled me up with it. We were inches apart. I could smell his cologne. Old Spice, Mary West had told me.

The thought of Mary, probably lying dead somewhere, did it. That and a surge of adrenaline. With the strength of true fear, I jerked the pipe out of Jake's hands and scrambled away from him.

I had maybe five seconds to avoid his pinning me and taking the pipe away, and I looked wildly around the room for some way to save myself. If I tried to hit him with the pipe, the blow would probably glance off his muscular torso. Then he'd not only kill me, he'd do it with gusto. There was no way I could make it to the door; he'd catch me in transit. Behind me was my desk and the wall.

I repeated a maneuver I'd tried in 1971, when two military policemen cornered me in a Presidio parking lot. I climbed: then it had been a car; now it was my desk. Watching Jake stride toward me, I remembered how ill-advised my simian gambit had been in 1971: the MPs had hauled me down and carried me to a compound of protesters, pending the arrival of federal marshalls.

Jake shook his head, apparently saddened that I would put him to so much trouble. I gripped the pipe with both hands, raising it like a baseball bat. It clanged against an overhead pipe, nearly jarring me off my feet. But it gave me an idea.

I began hammering at the maze of pipes, smashing them as hard as I could, desperately hoping to knock something loose. By the time Jake grabbed my legs and yanked me off the desk, my battering had produced results. Water began to drip, then spray around the room like a car wash out of control.

We ended up on the floor under a geyser of water that reminded me of a water canon I'd taken in the gut the day of the MPs. Jake scrambled to his feet, swearing. He had the pipe again, he was mad as hell, and I was lying there half blinded by spurting jets of water. I thought I was dogmeat.

The pipe rose inexorably, inch by inch. Ready to grovel for my life, I looked up at Jake. He was staring at his hands, the pipe arrested at a ninety degree angle from his body like a giant phallus. The caked portion had gotten wet, and the stain was reconstituting into blood.

Jake dropped the pipe, stumbling backward and shuddering at the dark smears on his fingers.

The overhead plumbing began to groan and boom, spitting icy water from a dozen new junctures. Parts of the heaving network slowly began to collapse, flushing water in every direction, making waterfalls of desktops, sweeping insect colonies to the floor.

I ducked one rank torrent in time to catch another full in the face. I spat out the metallic water, watching apprehensively as the pipes continued sinking, dropping o-rings and, squirting brownish cascades over bookcases, filing cabinets and—worst of all—my desk full of page proofs.

Jake gaped at the plumbing, his stained hands held fastidiously away from his body. I crawled on all fours toward the door, hoping to beat my retreat before he recalled his desire to perform a Final Edit on me.

I crawled smack into a pair of olive duck trousers. I looked up to see our short, barrel-shaped janitor running both hands over his brilliantined head. He surveyed the

mess, his eyes glistening with tears of frustration. *"Jesús
y María!"* he cried. *"Jesús y María!"*

I stood up, gripping the epaulets of his uniform and
panting, *"Him! He's* the one, Alfonsin!"

Alfonsin the janitor pulled me through the doorway, into
the outer office. He began swearing in such rapidfire Spanish that I caught only a fleeting reference to Jake's mother.

Jake Whittsen seemed oblivious to everything but the
hissing disaster overhead. In his haste to dash out of harm's
way, he ran right into me and Alfonsin.

Alfonsin stood on his toes and shook his fist at Jake.
Very red of face, he began shouting about the *"polizia."*
Jake shoved him aside, fleeing into the corridor.

Alfonsin slammed the inner office door and crossed angrily to the telephone.

As he dialed, Carla Sackett hurried in, announcing,
"There's water in the hall!" Another editor joined us with
the same announcement.

I sank into a Naugahyde couch. My adrenaline charge
had dissipated; I was again conscious of a stabbing headache. "A pipe burst."

By this time water was pouring through the space beneath the inner office door, swelling the pile of our worn
indoor-outdoor carpet, gurgling into the corridor.

Alfonsin slammed down the receiver, then charged out
of the room. I remained there, half-frozen in my soaked
sweater, to wait for the police.

36

IT TURNED OUT I'd been overly optimistic. When Alfonsin found me fleeing Jake in a room full of spraying water, he did not deduce, as I'd assumed a reasonable janitor would, that Jake was trying to kill me. He surmised that we'd been coping with an enormous plumbing problem. So when I told the agitated Colombian that Jake was "the one," Alfonsin supposed I meant the one who'd broken the pipes. That's why he'd menaced Jake with his fist and threatened him with the *polizia*.

But in fact, Alfonsin had not phoned the *polizia*—he'd called the water department. Then he'd rushed upstairs to turn off the water at the main line.

Meanwhile I sat ineffectually in the outer office, my clothes streaked with ill-smelling pipe effluvium and my head throbbing. I was saving my story for the police (I thought), so I snubbed the students gathering at the acrylic partition to gawk at the dangling, dripping pipes. I had no inkling of the truth until Larry Tchielowicz sloshed casually through the crowd, dropping onto the couch beside me.

"Jesus," he commented. "Whittsen was right; it's a mess down here." I was rendered speechless, and Larry, craning his neck to peer through the water-spotted acrylic, continued, "How'd it happen?"

" 'Whittsen was right!' Whittsen just tried to fucking kill me, and you're chitty-chatting with him?"

That got his attention. "Whittsen did what?"

I told him in a few invective-laced sentences what had happened.

I looked like a drowned rat, and no doubt smelled like one, too. I guess that didn't bother Larry. He folded me into his arms and squeezed most of the air out of my lungs. He didn't seem to want to let go, and I would have been in no hurry either, had I not required oxygen.

"You just let him walk out of here?"

"The janitor called the cops. I can't believe how long they're taking!"

That's when Alfonsin returned, leading a small army of towel-laden cafeteria workers. A few bilingual questions established the magnitude of our misunderstanding.

Larry bullied all spectators out of the office, then phoned Lieutenant Surgelato. He not only knew the number, but he immediately got through to the star quarterback himself.

The impromptu cleanup crew was noisily lamenting the extra work, so I didn't hear most of what Tchielowicz said. I did hear him reassure Surgelato, in a rather startled tone, "No, really—she's fine."

Tchielowicz rejoined me on the couch, explaining that he'd encountered a wringing wet Jake climbing into his squareback. Jake told him that a pipe had burst downstairs and that he was going home to change his clothes. The clever bastard had bought himself escape time.

Five minutes after Larry phoned him, Don Surgelato strode into the room. Unlike the two detectives with him, he didn't even glance at the water soaking into his wing-tips.

He stopped a few feet from the couch, stuffed his fists into his overcoat pockets, and frowned down at me. "You told me you were leaving your 'effing office 'even as we speak'!" he complained. "What the hell happened?"

But before I could begin, he observed, "You're wet!"

"I had to smash up the pipes to keep Jake from—"

Unfortunately, Alfonsin was in the outer office to hear my admission.

"Usted!" he seethed, advancing angrily.

Surgelato pushed him back, flashing a police ID. "Come on." He motioned for me to stand. "I'm not gonna let you catch pneumonia on top of a concussion. I'll drive you home. You can tell me about it after you get into dry clothes."

I didn't much like the idea of going home with Don Surgelato. Judging from the look on Tchielowicz's face, he didn't either.

37

My LANDLORD POPPED into the hallway, almost colliding with me. "Walter Mondale!" he bellowed.

Ben Bubniak, a beer-bellied man with long scraggles of yellow-gray hair and cheeks the color of clam broth, delighted in discovering new additions to the Trilateral Commission. He refused to consider the commission a social club where wealthy men basked in prestige while pretending to affect world politics. The Trilateral Commission was the tenth horn of the fourth beast of Revelations, and thus the last prophesied "government" to arise from the ashes of the Roman Empire.

"Mondale?" The thought of the ineffectual former Vice President triggering Armageddon brought a smile to my face.

"That's what they want you to think! Why do you think they took Jimmy Carter? And Gerald Ford?"

I patted his flannel-clad arm as I passed him. "They'll be recruiting Warren Burger next."

Don Surgelato peered beyond Ben into an apartment papered with science fiction and fantasy posters. He nodded, as though half-naked space warriors and fearsome aliens were exactly what he'd expected to see.

I flung open my apartment door. The perfume of unaired laundry and uncollected garbage mingled with the mildew smell of the narrow hallway. Home at last.

I crossed to the window, pounding on the sash till it rattled open. When I turned back to Surgelato, I found him expertly examining my lock. "It wasn't broken."

"Broken? Why should it have been—?"

"But this'd be an easy one to spring, with the right tools."

I surveyed the living room: clothes on the furniture, papers on the floor, drawers open and jumbled in my futile search for a pen with ink. "I'm afraid the place always looks like this. Worse, before exams."

I crossed into the bedroom, closing the door behind me. The first order of business was hiding my pot. The second was showering and putting on clean clothes. When I was done, I kicked some socks off the couch and resigned myself to Surgelato's presence.

He was sitting in the bay window on my library table, his hefty bottom on my intellectual property notes. "So what happened?"

"Jake Whittsen tried to kill me."

"Just tell the story. Let me draw the conclusions."

I told the story.

"Whittsen finds you holding the pipe?"

"Right."

"You fall off the chair. Whittsen tries to get the pipe away from you."

"He was going to—"

"Kill you? You're what, five three? He's six, six one. He must not have been trying very hard."

"I fought back. I used my wits."

The lieutenant snorted, glancing at his wristwatch. I guess he didn't think much of my wits. When he stood up, he noticed he'd been warming my class notes. "You hit the books pretty hard?"

"No harder than I have to."

"Number four—correction, number two—in your class."

"Not since I blew federal income tax."

Surgelato skimmed a page of my notes. "How do you study?"

"I look for a relationship, some fine point, I think the professor hasn't noticed. Then I milk it dry on the exam." I sighed. "Federal income tax was problem sets—no essay questions."

"Me," he mused, "I used to turn everything into lists. Memorize them."

"Susan Green memorized, but she didn't need to make lists; she remembered naturally." I rubbed my temples, trying not to whimper about my headache. "We were no match for her, any of us. Last year a bunch of students even got up a petition, demanding that her exam scores not be averaged into the grade curve."

"Twenty-two years since I graduated college and joined the force," Surgelato continued, as though I hadn't spoken. "Fifteen men under me now."

It sounded like an evening at the bath house.

He threw up his hands. "Okay! They'll have my butt if I don't pull Whittsen in!" His beetle-brows sank, obscuring his eyes. "But it doesn't smell right to me, so keep your back to the wall for a while, will you?"

After Surgelato left, I sat at the library table, looking out the bay window at streetcar cables and power lines.

I thought about what the lieutenant had said. Jake Whittsen is a big man, and I'm a small woman, and yet I'd kept him from striking me. I'd fought back, true; and I'd shown a little resourcefulness (whatever Surgelato might think). Even so, it almost seemed I'd been too lucky. Lucky, for one thing, that Jake had hesitated when I'd been most vulnerable, that he'd nearly swooned at the sight of blood on his hands. It was an odd reaction for a man who'd killed three people.

And yet, Jake had wrenched the pipe out of my hands. He must have meant to hit me with it.

I closed my eyes, considering our encounter. Whenever I'd had the pipe, Jake had come after me. Yet he'd blown at least two opportunities to kill me—once when I was on the ground and again after the deluge began. Maybe Surgelato was right. Maybe Jake hadn't been after me at all. Maybe he'd been after the pipe itself.

Fingerprints: maybe Jake knew, or thought he knew, who'd handled the murder weapon. Maybe he'd decided to protect that person by preventing me from turning the pipe over to the police. Maybe he'd meant to take the pipe away from me and ditch it somewhere.

But who would Jake go to such lengths to protect?

Melissa was the logical choice, of course. Maybe Susan had accused her of some kind of illegal arrangement with Clarence Day; maybe Melissa had felt compelled to kill her. I supposed she might have killed Henderson and Parker, too, for reasons beyond my ken.

But that cab driver had been right: the murders, the hiding of the weapon, would have been tricky for a noneditor. Melissa, who was not even a student, would have been doubly conspicuous around the office. It was hard to imagine Melissa standing on Greg's chair to get the pipe down, and even harder to imagine her replacing it, without someone seeing her. It was hard to imagine Susan and Henderson, and possibly Greg, ignoring her while they went about their business.

I kept coming back to that: the murderer must have been enough of a fixture around the office that Susan would continue editing, and Henderson continue snooping through my desk.

But who else, which editor, would Jake want to protect?

I lay my head on the table, feeling weak and ill. I could think of only one person to whom Jake had been sufficiently close, for whom he might harbor a sense of guilty chivalry.

Mary West had vanished after Greg Parker's body was discovered. I had considered it ominous, frightening; now it seemed suspicious. Maybe Jake had reason to believe Mary's fingerprints were on that pipe.

He was smart enough to know that if he kept his mouth shut, Surgelato would have to release him for lack of evidence. After all, it was no crime to grapple with someone over a lead pipe.

Protecting Mary West would be inconvenient for him, but only temporarily. And maybe he felt he owed her that much, for breaking her heart.

And like a damned fool, I had not only handled the murder weapon, I'd doused it with water. With luck, traces of blood remained. But it would be a miracle if any fingerprints had survived my act of heroism.

38

LARRY PHONED TO ask how I felt (and, I think, to find out whether Surgelato was still there), but I decided not to tell him my theory. He'd seen my hurt pride the day Mary had announced she'd bedded Jake, and he'd heard from her (at least once) that Melissa had found us in a compromising position. I didn't want him writing off my suspicions as a lingering tenderness for Jake.

A little later, Surgelato phoned to say they'd taken Jake into custody. "He says he saw you with the pipe and assumed you were the murderer." He paused to allow me a moment of outrage. "He says he tried to get the pipe away from you so he could bring it to us."

Jake Whittsen, Model Citizen. I was sufficiently irritated to tell Surgelato that Susan's aunt had ruined Jake's brother-in-law's career.

Ten minutes later, two police inspectors arrived to take me to "the Hall."

Surgelato was clearly furious with me. His nostrils

twitched, his lips hardly moved when he spoke. "It didn't occur to you to mention this Koening thing to me sooner?"

I shrugged. My head was throbbing, my hair seemed to weigh ten pounds.

"I could have had my men on it. Tossed it on the red herring heap by now!" He paced beneath the photo of himself in a champagne-soaked football jersey. "We can't hold Whittsen without charging him, and we can't let him go till we investigate his brother-in-law's damned lawsuit!" He stopped beneath the portrait; twenty-two years had made his face tougher, jowlier. "Goddam it! I'm gonna have to arrest him for murder!"

He finally let me slink away. I went to my parents' flat, where my mother railed at me for cooperating with "the local fascist Gestapo (and after what they did to those poor gay men the other night!)."

The next morning, Jake Whittsen's noble face reproached me from every Civic Center newsstand. I cut class, returning to my parents' apartment to watch the news on their ancient, snowy television. I watched Surgelato push away microphones with a gruff "No comment." I watched Dean Sorenson solemnly read a statement, "regretting the impossibility of any large institution's being able to protect against the random violence of a deviant member." What a crude joke Mary West could have made of that!

I made the mistake of going to my afternoon class, and was rousted out of it by the dean's secretary. I ended up back in the dean's office, surrounded by his frowning busts.

Dean Sorenson informed me that it would take several weeks for "the crew" to scrape away the sodden carpeting and wet pegboard of the law review office. He stuck out his lower lip and regarded the bust of Alexander Hamilton. "I think the committee has more or less decided to leave the floor bare and install vending machines down there. You know, turn it into a small student lounge. Microwaves, candy machines, what have you." He glanced at me, then returned to Hamilton's ill-tempered profile. "I'm sure you're aware students complain about the privileges we accord law review—not that you don't deserve them. On the contrary. But I think turning over the basement office would be a pleasantly democratic gesture, don't you?"

"Where are we supposed to work?"

"That, my dear, is the good news!" He rubbed his long hands together. "The faculty has agreed to share its library with you!" He waited for an expression of gratitude I couldn't quite muster. "You may have to be more, uh, subdued than the basement office required you to be. But, from the standpoint of collegial relations between students and faculty, why, I think we can regard the water damage as a blessing in disguise!"

It was so well disguised that none of my fellow editors recognized it.

Whenever a faculty member entered the small fourth-floor library, we had to relinquish our wing chairs and step into the stifling corridor to discuss business. Only in the late evening, when the professors had returned to their Marin County homes, did their library finally become "ours."

When that happened, the new "office" was definitely more pleasant than the old. There were walls of leather-bound legal reporters, oak tables to spread manuscripts on, supple wingchairs with plump ottomans, and, best of all, windows. The view wasn't much, flophouses mostly, but windows meant natural light. And unlike other windows on the top two floors, the library windows weren't bolted shut (apparently they didn't worry about faculty members leaping to their deaths, or maybe they bolted them only during tenure hearings). The windows opened outward over deep casement ledges where pigeons could be heard tapping and cooing. After a year in the basement, fresh air seemed the ultimate luxury.

By week's end, we'd managed to evolve an evening work schedule, and most of the editors, still depressed about the murders and shocked about Jake, began to congregate in the faculty library after dinner to drink coffee (we'd moved the urn upstairs), work, and talk. Even Hatty McPherson returned to the fold. And Mary West came back, claiming that the discovery of Parker's body had "scared the crap out of her," and that she'd decided to leave town till the murderer was safely in jail. She made no apology for not having told her fellow editors—possible murderers all—where to find her; and she showed no surprise or sorrow over Jake's arrest.

With tensions still running high, Mary's explanation of her absence was accepted without question, though more than one editor expressed irritation at her thoughtlessness. Even Larry Tchielowicz seemed satisfied with her excuse.

And while everyone else showed a relieved greediness for Mary West's company and a renewed appreciation of her élan, I began to notice the malice in her wit. And I knew Mary could see what no one else did—that I no longer trusted her.

39

THE MURDERS HAD been "solved," the "killer" was in jail, the patio was devoid of reporters, security had been reduced to a single pair of brownshirts in the lobby, and our editors were finally beginning to receive job offers. Evening conversation in the faculty library featured the law student version of that boys' game, Mine Is Bigger ("You're clerking at the Court of Appeal? I'm clerking at the *Supreme* Court!"). Most of the editors had already cashed in the résumé value of being on law review; getting them to proof galleys for the spring issue and edit manuscripts for the summer issue was more trouble than the articles were worth, in my opinion. But the faculty, whom we encountered all too frequently in the small library, was adamant that we "rehabilitate our reputation" by keeping the review on schedule. So I wheedled, nagged, and blustered several hundred more hours of work from the editors.

That's why it was such a blow to our morale when the fully edited articles were stolen the morning they were to go to the printer. The fact that we'd done the work at all, with three of our editors dead and a fourth awaiting trial, had been a triumph of tradition over adversity. Even if I succeeded in convincing the editors to redo the work, the summer issue would be months late, and the faculty was sure to harass us every step of the way.

I was the one who discovered that the parcel of articles, and all of our office copies, were missing. And I was the one who called an emergency editors' meeting and announced to the small group (so few of us left, it seemed) that what murder had not done, thievery had.

The editors stared at me in mute disbelief. Hatty moaned. Carla Sackett covered her face with her hands. Tchielowicz stood up. No one spoke. Not until Mary West erupted, "Who did it? Goddam it, Willa! Who did it?"

She was silhouetted against an open window, looking rather wide of hip in her tunic sweater. Behind her, startled pigeons took wing.

Harold Scharr stepped between her and the rest of us, his arm extended as if to embrace her. She pushed the arm away. "My original was with the office copies!"

Mary's had been one of the stolen articles. She'd been justifiably proud of it, too, asking me a dozen times whether she'd have her reprints in time to mail them with her résumé before the July bar exam.

"You know who took them, don't you, Willa?"

"How would I know that?"

"You know a lot of things!" Her tone raised the hairs on the back of my neck.

She was partly right, though; I did have my suspicions. When an influx of professors scattered the editors, I walked resolutely down the hall.

If I'd stopped to think things through, maybe I could

have prevented a murder. But the theft was a knife in my back, and I wanted to challenge the person I believed had planted it there.

I knocked at her door, then tried the knob. I found her hunched over a cup of fruit salad. She glared at me across her tidy desk, then dropped her plastic fork and pushed the salad away.

"Stealing the articles was contemptible! You're contemptible!"

Professor Miles straightened her spine and pulled back the corners of her mouth in her best Bette Davis manner. "Please leave this office at once, Ms. Jansson. Before I call security and have you ejected."

Her eyelids were wrinkled, wine-colored with age. Her skin looked like turtle hide overlain with pink makeup. I hated her. "You couldn't bear Susan's having short-changed you in the editor's note, could you?"

"I will not dignify your accusations with a response."

"I assumed you'd lied about your degrees, and that was why Susan had omitted them. But they're real enough, aren't they, all those expensive pieces of parchment? And you felt slighted. Your prodigious ego was bruised because we weren't contrite enough. So you went looking for a way to do us mischief. You even searched our desks looking for scandal!"

She remained perfectly immobile, but outrage glittered in her eyes.

I walked out and slammed the door. A few paces down the hall, Harold Scharr was white as a ghost in his midnight-blue suit.

I turned away from him and crossed to a nearby restroom. Hatty McPherson stood near the door, but I gave

her such a sour look that she didn't speak to me. Alone in
the ladies' room, I broke down and cried.

40

WHEN I FINALLY emerged, I found Harold leaning
against the wall opposite the door.

"Hi," he said gently.

"Hi. Sorry I stomped off. I wasn't in the mood to talk."

"I could see that. In fact, I made Mary West find a
different restroom." He cupped a solicitous hand under
my elbow. "Want some coffee?"

We went down the block to a cafeteria with dusty plastic
flowers on the tables. I chose the place because our fellow
editors avoided it. I'd been there once with Henderson;
he'd owed me lunch and couldn't think of a cheaper place
to take me.

"Henderson said he was going to go to work for Clarence Day. Did you know that, Harold?"

He emptied an envelope of NutraSweet into a stained
Melmac coffee cup. "Actually, he got a call from a piggo
Wall Street firm the morning he died—"

"Wailes, Roth?"

"Right." He took a sip, grimacing.

"That was the job Henderson really wanted, wasn't it? With Wailes, Roth?"

"All I know is, Day pays thirty-five; Wailes, Roth pays sixty-five." Harold shrugged. "But Day did make Henderson an offer. I heard Lady Jane say so."

"You did?"

"Mm-hm." He reached across the table and intercepted my hand before it reached my bangs. "She was talking to Susan. It was after that speech she gave at Malhousie, the day—"

I libidinously inhaled a nearby diner's sidestream cigarette smoke. "The day Susan was killed?"

He frowned. "That's right. Susan and Henderson and Lady Jane were at Susan's desk, and Lady Jane said Henderson was coming to work for them and that she wanted Susan's 'honest assessment,' she called it, of some of the other editors she'd interviewed."

"Who else interviewed there?"

"Who didn't? Greg did, so did Hatty and Mary. Carla Sackett too, I think."

I drank some gritty coffee. "I suppose Susan was her usual honest self?"

"Oh she was tactful, but basically she said that Hatty was nervous as a cat and Mary twice as lazy. Henderson backed her up, of course. Unfortunately Mary and Hatty walked into the outer office and heard the whole thing. In fact, when I left, Hatty had that night-of-the-living-dead look she gets—you know the one—and Mary was about to go give Susan shit."

Mary was persistent when she wanted something, and it looked as though what she'd wanted from the Days was a job. I remembered Clarence Day complaining, that day on his patio, that "the West girl" had been driving him crazy.

Harold brushed some crumbs off the table and leaned closer. "I think I know who you suspect of the murders— not Jake, I know that. But one person you might not have considered is Greg. You're assuming the dead are all innocent, but I'd put my money on Parker, I really would. He could have killed Susan and Henderson—"

"Then killed himself? The cops agree with you, I think. They weren't very happy about arresting Jake."

"But you don't agree?"

"Greg was such a cupcake!"

"An ill-used cupcake. I wouldn't be a bit surprised if he resented us all for treating him like a germ." There was remorse and self-condemnation in Harold's tone. He worked a strip of napkin into a tight twist.

"I don't know. Parker seemed so oblivious— Think of all the times he tagged along after we made a show of not wanting him."

Harold flicked the bit of paper off the table. "Ginny Miles didn't steal those articles, Willa."

"Harold!"

"And I hate to say this, I really do. But I think you owe her an apology."

"What about the time I caught her snooping around the office? And she hates me! You know that!"

"Oh, no doubt about it! And I'm sure she was snooping around looking for some dirt—on you personally." He slid his long fingers over my hand. "But think about it! Ginny used to be the law review's faculty advisor! We publish her articles all the time! Her own prestige as an author, as a member of Malhousie's exalted faculty, depends in part on the law review! You know how the faculty feels about the review's reputation! Ginny might do something to embarrass *you*, but she'd never sabotage the review itself!"

I pulled my hand out from under his. "Well, who else would want to steal those articles?"

"I don't know."

"You *like* Miles, don't you?" I accused him.

He took another brave sip of coffee. "Like her? No. But she treats me with respect, most days. And she pays me on time."

"I won't apologize!"

"That's up to you. I've done my duty."

He left a couple of dollars on the table and walked out.

41

THE FACULTY LIBRARY was deserted, except for Mary West. She was rummaging through a stack of books and class notes I'd left on the corner table, near the library phone.

"What the hell are you looking for?"

She glanced up, showing no surprise or embarrassment,

then went back to pawing through my papers. "Henderson used to swear you did drugs. He was always going through your desk trying to find some. He'd have made a great narc."

I sat on a window ledge opposite her. "You won't find any drugs in there!"

"I'm just being thorough. I've looked everywhere else. My article is definitely gone." She folded her arms and put her head down on the oak table. A shaft of sunlight, sparkling with tiny dust motes, bathed her head and shoulders.

I tried to feel sorry for her, but it was like trying to pity a coiled snake.

I shifted on the ledge, looking past the pigeon-spotted casement at the gridlocked traffic below.

I was startled out of my reverie when the telephone beside Mary began to ring. Mary, head still on her arms, didn't bother to answer it.

I walked to the corner table, noticing that the hair on Mary's arms gleamed red-blond in the sun. Her watch read 11:05.

I picked up the phone, murmuring, "Law review. Willa Jansson." I could smell Mary's scent, an uncharacteristically flowery one.

It was Dean Sorenson. "Ah, Ms. Jansson, so glad I caught you!"

He usually sent a lackey to fetch me to his office. What could a phone call mean?

"Uh, let me get right to the point, my dear." The dean getting right to the point: it had to be a bad sign. "Virginia Miles was here to see me earlier this morning."

Damn that woman!

"And uh, she was a trifle upset by a misunderstanding over some law review articles?"

"I was a trifle upset myself."

"I understand completely, my dear! I've been discussing it with your Mr. Scharr, and I think he's quite justified in characterizing this distressing event as a matter for the police. And you certainly have my assurance that the entire faculty stands behind the review! You may call on us at any time to help in whatever way we can!"

He paused for my obligatory "Thank you."

"But uh, Ms. Jansson, as for this other small matter . . . Knowing you as I do, I felt I might assure Professor Miles of my absolute confidence in your ability to rise above the shock and pain of the moment and extend the olive branch to her, *sua sponte!*"

Damn!

"Ms. Jansson? May I consider the matter settled?"

What could I say but "Yes." I slammed down the receiver, adding, with greater sincerity, "Shit!"

Mary West, still seated beside the phone, grabbed my wrist. "Was that about the articles?"

"No! Let go of me!" I tried to jerk free, but I couldn't break Mary's grip.

She looked up at me, her cheeks mottling. "You're lying! You know something you're not telling me!"

"Oh that's fucking beautiful! *Me* lying!" I tried again to yank my wrist free. "And Jake rotting in jail to protect you!"

She stood up, her fingers digging deeper into my flesh. "You're crazy! What are you talking about?"

"Why's he doing it, Mary? What does he know—?"

"He knows how to get me pregnant!" Her eyes, already

puffy, began to glisten with angry tears. "But not how to forget his ball breaker of a wife!"

Pregnant! It explained so much: Mary's sudden preference for baggy clothes; Jake's remark, which I'd thought figurative, about Mary's knitting baby booties; and most of all, his reason for protecting a woman he knew, or at least suspected, was a murderess.

"That bastard!" she continued. "It would have been damned convenient for him if I was out of the way!"

"Come on! You don't think he wanted to kill you?"

"Yes. No. I don't know. With everybody getting bumped off around here, how should I know?"

"And that scared you into hiding?"

She nodded.

"I don't believe you. And goddam it, if you don't let go—"

"Just tell me what happened to my article! Who was that on the phone?"

I heard the click of wooden heels. Hatty McPherson pushed through the door, eyes darting, hair disheveled, her usual neurotic self.

Mary released my arm, blotting her eyes with a woolly sleeve.

Hatty quavered, "Did Professor Miles find you? She was looking for you a while ago. I think she's mad about something!"

Mary pushed past me, hurriedly leaving the library.

Hatty continued crossly, "You don't expect us to edit all those articles again, do you, Willa? We have to start studying for finals! It wouldn't be fair!"

I refrained—barely—from knocking her to the floor as I passed her.

I walked slowly down the hall, past the restrooms, past Gunnar Haas' office. Sunlight poured through a bolted window at the end of the corridor, baking the worn carpet. Turning the corner, I was vaguely aware of staccato car horns on the street below.

I hesitated in front of the professor's door. Less than an hour earlier, I'd burst in to find her eating fruit salad in ill-tempered solitude. I supposed my accusation had been hasty—Harold had a point about Miles' prestige being tied to the law review's reputation. But goddam her! Complaining to the dean had been calculated to make trouble, not peace.

I tapped on the frosted panel. "Professor Miles?"

No answer.

I tried the door, hoping I'd find it locked.

No such luck: it opened.

The professor's swivel chair was angled away from the desk, facing the back corner. From the doorway I could see only the silk bow of her blouse and her wrinkled claw, resting palm down on the arm rest.

"Professor?" I couldn't keep an undercurrent of anger out of my voice.

She didn't reply.

I stepped around to the side of her desk, furious that she would summon me and then refuse to speak to me.

Her head was lolling on her shoulder, a pouch of wrinkled flesh trapped between her collar and her chin. Her eyes were open, staring straight ahead in glazed shock. In the light of the corner windows, I could see that they were pale blue, that her lashes were caked with brown mascara. Her skin looked waxy, almost clammy, under streaks of orange rouge. And on her right temple, partially covered by singed hair, was a raw, star-shaped wound.

I whispered, "Professor Miles?"

I touched her shoulder. Her body began sliding sideways across the high back of her chair. The motion jerked her head to the opposite shoulder, and her right hand fell from her lap to the seat cushion. Beneath it, the burgundy leather was black with the contents of her relaxed bladder.

I caught her before she toppled; her shoulder felt bony and frail beneath the silk of her blouse. As I righted her, the chair swiveled several degrees back toward the desk. Something fell from her lap to the floor.

I looked down. It was a small gun.

And suddenly a woman shouted, "Freeze!"

A uniformed policewoman filled the doorway, legs spread wide, knees slightly bent, gun hand firmly braced against her forearm.

42

SURGELATO WAS TAKING no chances. Every time he sent a team of homicide inspectors in to question me, they read me my rights over again. I probably should have let a lawyer do my talking for me, but after three years of law school, it would have seemed like hiring a hippie to smoke my pot for me.

Sometimes the questions were about me: Did I kill Professor Miles? Did I kill Susan Green, John Henderson, and Greg Parker?

Sometimes the questions were about the professor: Did she have any enemies? Did she have any reason to kill herself? Could she have killed Susan Green, John Henderson, and Greg Parker?

I answered as coherently as I was able. I'd never seen a dead person before. I couldn't stop thinking about her glassy blue eyes.

After the third team of detectives had asked me the same questions I'd answered for the preceding two teams, Surgelato himself stepped into the room. He motioned for the detectives to leave.

I disengaged my fingers from my bangs, spreading them a few inches from my nose. "They sprayed something on my hand, then they wiped it off with Q-tips. Will that tell them I didn't fire the gun?"

Surgelato frowned at my hand. "Dilute nitric acid solution. It picks up traces of gunpowder, yes."

"Good!" The hand trembled slightly as I lowered it to my lap.

Surgelato extended a pack of Kools to me.

I said no before I realized what I had done; the habit part of my addiction was apparently behind me. But the craving wasn't; I watched him light a cigarette and I bled to join him.

He turned a chair around and straddled it, resting his forearms on what should have been the back. "We want to help you—I mean that sincerely. But you're not telling us everything you know.'' Cigarette smoke streamed from his mouth and nose.

''I'm trying, but I can't seem to think! I didn't kill her!''

''Did you have any reason to?''

''No! I argued with her, but I wouldn't have—''

''Argued?''

''About some articles I thought she'd stolen! But you don't kill someone for screwing up a publication deadline!''

''Slow down. What articles?''

I explained about the missing manuscripts. ''I was sure it was the professor—she always acted like she hated me! So I went to her office.''

''And?''

I described my *J'Accuse*—and its aftermath.

''Dean Sorenson insisted I apologize. Him and Harold Scharr. Lieutenant, where did that policewoman come from?''

Surgelato toyed with his cigarette pack, his head bowed so I couldn't see his face. ''Officer Winkle was dispatched at ten fifty-six to investigate a possible theft. Call came from Miles' office; that's all we know about it.''

''Theft? Of the law review articles?''

He lifted his head, meeting my eyes. ''We don't know.''

''Was there gunpowder on Professor Miles' hand?''

''Yeah. Could have been suicide, we're not ruling that out. But you put a gun into someone's hand right after it's been fired and you're bound to get a little gunpowder on it. We're checking the prints; we'll have a better idea later today.''

I scooted my chair closer to his. "What about Jake Whittsen? If this was murder—"

"Let me worry about Whittsen."

"But I was thinking, maybe he's protecting—" I stopped myself; I'd already made one accusation that day, and look where it had gotten me.

"Yeah? Protecting who?" He tapped a Kool out of the pack and offered it to me.

I took it; it felt right, between my fingers. "I don't know if it makes any sense."

He struck a match, shielding the small flame. "Talk to me, Willa. Let me decide what makes sense." The match burned down to his fingers and he dropped it. "I want to help you."

I never did light the cigarette, but I did talk to him. I told him every theory I'd ever entertained, everything I'd seen anybody do that might have any bearing on anything. I told him about Professor Miles prowling the law review office; I told him about Gunnar Haas and his manuscript; I told him about Jane Day searching the filing cabinet; about Susan's list of Clarence Day's properties. I repeated what I'd already told him about Mrs. Koenig and Jake Whittsen and the Bonominis; I told him I'd seen Day with Melissa Whittsen on Christmas Eve; I told him Jake had had an affair with Mary West, and that he might be protecting her because she was going to have his baby.

My mother would have disowned me if she'd heard the half of it.

The only thing I didn't tell him was that John Henderson had been checking up on Larry Tchielowicz right before he died.

Surgelato sat there smoking, and occasionally glancing

at a mirrored panel to our left. It didn't occur to me until the end of my soliloquy that the panel was a one-way mirror. Surgelato's underlings must have been impressed at the torrent of information he'd unleashed; maybe they even poured champagne over his head.

When I stopped talking, Surgelato dropped what must have been his sixth cigarette, grinding it out with a polished black shoe. He stood up, bowing slightly. "Thank you."

He left the room and was replaced, two or three minutes later, by another team of detectives. One of them handed me a piece of paper on a clipboard. The other clicked on a tape recorder, saying, "Please read this waiver and state for the record that you understand you have the right—"

But I had a better idea. "I want to talk to my lawyer."

The detective nearly dropped the tape recorder. He and his partner retreated to a corner to do some frantic mumbling. One of them went out, returning a few minutes later to say, "All right. We'll call your lawyer for you. Who is it?"

"Clarence Day."

His eyes bugged out.

"Please ask Mr. Day to come here right away."

The detectives exchanged "uh-oh" glances. They seemed reluctant to report the development to their boss.

43

CLARENCE DAY ARRIVED forty minutes later. A uniformed cop ushered him into the drab little room, then left us alone.

Day took my hand, looking as kindly and concerned as a man in a thousand-dollar suit can look.

He spoke *de haute en bas*. "How can I help?"

"As I talk to the lieutenant, I keep coming back to you and your wife, over and over again. Your wife was at Malhousie the day Susan died and she's been lurking around there ever since, not to mention singing in the same choir as Greg and interviewing half the law review staff. And you—you represented Susan's aunt, you sued Jake's brother-in-law, you spent Christmas Eve with his wife. You and your wife are making yourselves conspicuous. How come?"

Day was an imposing figure in his charcoal pinstripes and maroon silk tie. His face was pink and freshly shaved, his silver hair was perfectly cut, his nails were manicured and buffed to a high gloss. "Ms. Jansson, my wife and I are always conspicuous. Like it or not, we're public figures."

"But why isn't your wife off campaigning? Why is she always hanging around Malhousie? I know it's her alma mater, but it's not a top ten law school. Why isn't she interviewing *Stanford* law students, buddying around with *their* faculty?"

I wasn't sure where I was heading, but I certainly had Clarence Day's attention—and doubtless that of the detectives on the other side of the mirror.

Day answered mildly, "Does she need a reason?"

"Then tell me, what does the Koenig case have to do with all this? Everyone involved in that case seems to have a representative on the scene—the plaintiff's niece, the defendant's brother-in-law, the lawyer's wife."

Day brushed nonexistent lint from his sleeve. "Let me ask you, Ms. Jansson, did you summon me here because you need legal counsel?"

"You wouldn't accept a criminal case—you're a personal injury lawyer."

"That's right."

"But you came to see me."

"I'm acquainted with you. And I might be able to recommend someone."

"How did you feel about losing the Koenig case?"

"I was sorry for Mrs. Koenig, but Walter Bonomini was an extremely handsome and sympathetic young man— and juries do respond to that."

"Right after you lost that case, you bought some land from Mrs. Koenig."

He raised a venerable white brow.

"You also bought land from J. H. Van Heusen and George K. Millar."

A chill crept into his voice. "You're very well informed."

"No, Susan Green was. At first we thought she must be collecting evidence against you to present to the state bar, but really, those land dealings make you look like a saint!" I knotted my fingers into my hair. "If you'd written that list of properties yourself, it couldn't have made you look any—"

I broke off and stared. "That's *it*! *You* wrote the list! You *wanted* the police to focus on the Koenig case! You knew Susan was Mrs. Koenig's niece because she was in court with Mrs. Koenig every day of the trial. And you knew Bonomini's brother-in-law was on the law review staff because you've been seeing Melissa Whittsen—"

"What? Seeing whom?"

"Bonomini's sister."

Clarence Day shook his head. "I haven't been 'seeing' her, as you put it. I met her once, at a public restaurant, because I got a phone call to go there—"

"A phone call? But you were in church, or you should have been. Listening to your wife sing in the choir."

"I'm not Catholic. I attend the morning service at—" He looked irritated. "Not that it's any of your business."

"You found out Jake was related to Walter Bonomini, so you planted that list of properties in the law review office. Anyone could forge Susan's writing—she wrote in green capital letters, of all the stupid affectations." I sat up straight. "In fact, that's what your wife was doing in the law review office that day: she was planting the list so the cops would find it and start investigating the Koenig connection!''

Clarence Day leaned back in the chair Surgelato had recently occupied. ''An interesting line of thought. Someone (not Jane, I'm sorry to say) plants this list, and sooner or later the police decide that Mr. Whittsen has committed some sort of, what? Revenge killing?''

''Your wife planted the list!''

''And in doing so—as I understand your scenario—connected herself and me to several murders. What could be more likely?''

''You were already connected—Susan was reading a draft of your wife's student article when she died!''

''Yes, she was,'' Day acknowledged. ''She was curious to see how the editing techniques of your law review had evolved over the years. She and Jane were discussing it, and at her request Jane brought her an edited draft, for general comparison purposes.''

I shook my head. ''Maybe a jury would believe that, but no editor would. 'Editing techniques!' We do whatever it takes to make the manuscripts coherent! That's enough trouble without worrying about what editors did fifteen years ago. No, if Susan told you that, she was lying.''

''I'm not qualified to pass judgment on Ms. Green's veracity.'' He seemed consummately relaxed on the scarred, wobbly chair.

''If she wanted to see an edited draft of your wife's article, she had some other reason.'' I rubbed my temples. My landlord had a theory about fluorescent rays interfering with brain waves; I was beginning to believe it.

''Mr. Day, did you know that Susan's article was about campaign financing disclosure laws, just like your wife's?

Your wife's is completely out of date now, but Susan must have read it when she researched her article. It's odd that she didn't cite it. Don't you think it's odd?''

"It may indicate sloppy research on Ms. Green's part, but I don't know why I should find it 'odd.' '' He stifled a smile. "I'm sure you mean to tell me, Ms. Jansson."

"Susan didn't do sloppy research. Susan had a photographic memory, and she was excruciatingly thorough. And Malhousie's law review published your wife's article—Susan should have felt a chauvinistic duty to cite it."

Clarence Day glanced at his Rolex. "I'm afraid I'll have to be—"

"Wait a minute, let me think about this. Henderson and Mary edited Susan's article. I wonder if *they* knew why she didn't cite it."

"If you'd like me to recommend a criminal attorney—"

"Funny nobody mentioned it to *me*; I *am* senior articles editor! Unless—!" I reached out and clutched his sleeve. "What if they *agreed* to keep the reason a secret? What if something about your wife's article reflected badly on the law review?"

"Ms. Jansson, really!" He brushed my hand off his elegant pinstripes. "I'm afraid I'll have to leave you to your conjectures—"

"*Plagiarism!* Of course! That's why Susan asked to see an edited draft of your wife's article! To see what it looked like under the red ink!"

Clarence Day stood up and began patting his pockets, apparently untroubled by my insight.

"Let's say that fifteen years ago, your wife plagiarized an article in the law review's slush pile of rejected manuscripts—some article she was sure would never see the printed page. Your wife was already president of half the student organizations on campus; she probably didn't have time to write her own article. And she probably counted on 'her' article being so thoroughly edited that the real author would never recognize it. But say the original ended up in some minor review. Say Susan ran across it years later and noticed the similarity to your wife's—phrases, syntax, things that would leap out at you if you had a photographic memory! Maybe Susan began to suspect that your wife had committed—''

''Plagiarism!'' Day mused, still patting his pockets. ''And you're suggesting that Jane murdered—what? three people?—to conceal—''

''Well it's not pederasty, but think about it! Your wife's running for public office. A charge like that would undermine public confidence in her honesty, in her intellectual ability, in her sense of fair play!''

''Oh, I agree.'' He extracted a business card from his breast pocket. ''Look what cheating on college exams did to poor Ted Kennedy's career.''

He handed me the card. It read Winship, McAuliffe, Potter & Tsieh, Criminal Law.

''I won't keep you much longer, Mr. Day. Please give me another moment.''

With a resigned sigh, he sat back down.

''You say Susan Green asked your wife for that draft of her article. I believe you. And I believe your wife accepted Susan's explanation of why she wanted it. Your wife had never done any stylistic edits—as executive editor, she'd corrected form, not substance. She wouldn't realize there's no such thing as an editing technique. And after fifteen years, she certainly wouldn't worry about anyone accusing her of plagiarism.''

"I don't want to appear rude, Ms. Jansson, but I have other matters to attend to. And we do seem to be covering the same ground.''

"The point is, the draft proved to Susan that your wife had plagiarized another article. And that put Susan in a bind. Our review had published your wife's article—and publishing plagiarized material doesn't do much for a law review's reputation! On the other hand, Susan was too fastidious to cite a plagiarized article! So what could she do? Nothing, really—except confide in the two people who were editing her own article. Susan was proud of her intellect; she wouldn't let Mary West and John Henderson suspect her of poor research. But she might ask them to keep your wife's transgression a secret—to protect the law review.''

Clarence Day was looking at his Rolex again.

"Now John Henderson, he had built-in incentive to keep the secret: he had every expectation of being hired by your law firm. But Mary West—she had expensive tastes and no income. And maybe it occurred to her to come to you and hammer out a little business arrangement—''

"West! My only dealings with a Ms. West have been to assure her—repeatedly—that we do not anticipate hiring another associate.''

"Susan was murdered the day her article was published. Why that day, I wonder? Because somebody in particular read it?''

"Ms. Jansson, surely you don't require my presence for this—''

"Virginia Miles! Of course! She was the law review's

faculty advisor when your wife was an editor! If anyone remembered your wife's article, it would have been Miles! Oh my god, and she was furious with Susan for editing some of her accomplishments out of an editor's note! She must have read Susan's article and then taunted Susan for not citing your wife's on the same subject! She could be so damned unpleasant; she probably made a point of disparaging Susan's research! Susan couldn't have stood that!''

''I bow to your superior knowledge of Ms. Green, but I really must go.'' He got to his feet, extending his hand in farewell.

''No, wait! Say Susan asks the professor to come down to the law review office later that afternoon. She gets your wife's draft ready to show to her. And then she makes a serious—even fatal—mistake. She finds herself alone in the office with Mary West and she tells Mary what she's going to do. She tells Mary she can't have Professor Miles repeating her accusations to other faculty members; that she's not willing to protect your wife's reputation—or even the law review's—at the expense of her own.''

''Winship, McAuliffe''—Clarence Day pointed to the business card I still held in my hand—''is an excellent firm. I encourage you to phone Roland Tsieh if you—''

''But see, if your wife's secret becomes public knowledge, Mary West is in big trouble. She not only loses her extra income, but your wife might tell the police Mary's been blackmailing her. Your wife would have nothing to lose at that point—plagiarism's not a criminal offense. And Mary—well, they don't let you practice law if you've been convicted of blackmail. She'd not only lose her blackmail income, but her career would go down the drain.''

Day remained standing, his hand still extended. Vertical lines appeared between his brows.

"As for John Henderson, he must not have realized the motive for Susan's murder; he must not have known Mary was blackmailing your wife. He must have bragged to Mary that he'd gotten a better job offer and that he wouldn't be working for your firm, after all. And once Mary realized he'd lost his incentive to keep your wife's secret— Well, if the truth came out at that point, the police might put two and two together and arrest Mary."

Clarence Day turned away. He was opening the door when I added, "But you and your wife killed Greg Parker!"

He turned around, his hand still on the door knob. His close-shaven cheeks were pale, his face impassive.

"Your wife ran into Greg on her way to choir practice, didn't she?" I noticed my tone was apologetic. "Greg got off the Polk Street bus at North Point, and it's a six- or seven-block walk from there to Peter and Paul's. Your wife had seen him at other choir practices; she'd even interviewed him for a job. She recognized him and offered him a lift—I notice she does her own driving. He'd probably read your wife's article in our law review, hoping to impress her. He might have said any number of things that convinced her he knew the big secret, too. Two people were already dead. Even though your wife wasn't responsible, she couldn't afford to have anyone connecting her, even inadvertently, with those murders."

Clarence Day sighed ever so wearily. "Roland Tsieh is an excellent criminal lawyer," he repeated. Then he left the room.

44

SURGELATO ENTERED THE room with gale force. He stood before my chair, hands on his hips, head thrust forward like a vulture's.

"What did you think of my theory?" I ventured.

Through paralyzed lips, he muttered, "What theory is that?"

"Clarence Day—"

"I hear you sent for him."

If Surgelato wasn't going to mention the one-way mirror, I thought I'd better not, either. The thing violated my Fourth and Fifth Amendment rights, so he was likely to be touchy about it.

For the sake of appearances, therefore, I recapitulated my conversation with Day, concluding, "Virginia Miles was the only person left who could shed light on the motive for all the murders. Mary must have been planning all along to kill her! She must have been biding her time, waiting for the perfect opportunity! And today when I accused the professor of theft— Why, even if the police did see through the phony suicide, they'd suspect *me*, not her!"

Surgelato listened, face turned away and one wing-tipped foot braced against the seat of a folding chair. Judging from the play of his jaw muscles, he was grinding his molars to the nub.

I waited several minutes for him to speak. I began to wonder if the session would end with a rubber hosing.

Finally he kicked away the folding chair, waving his beef-flank of an arm. "What are the police here for?"

I decided this was a rhetorical question.

He bent at the waist, his face less than a foot from mine. "You couldn't let the *pros* question Day! No—it's better for a little princess of a law student to do it!"

Searching for something to say in my own defense, I realized I'd told Day everything I knew about the murders, while he'd admitted nothing to me. I tried to press through the back slats of my chair.

The lieutenant straightened, waved his arm some more, then stomped out. For another two hours, I remained alone in the overlit, unadorned room. I couldn't have felt sorrier for myself if I'd been the Count of Monte Cristo.

A uniformed policeman finally accompanied me out of the building and into the icy wind (San Francisco's bi-weekly hour of balmy weather had passed). He offered to drive me wherever I wanted to go, and I asked him for a ride to my parents' flat. The cop parked the big black and white car half on the street and half on the curb, less then five feet from the apartment building door. When I went inside, he remained there like a conspicuous watchdog.

I didn't tell my mother where I'd spent my afternoon. It was too long a story, and she wouldn't have approved of my cooperating with the cops. I told her Professor Miles had killed herself, but I didn't elaborate.

Mother was distressed by the news. "Imagine that poor woman's burden of despair! Working so hard and so long, fighting for every ounce of respect she could wring from her colleagues!" Mother wiped away a tear. "How often do you hear about a *male* law professor killing himself?"

I decided it would be unseemly to say, "Not often enough!"

Mother happened to glance out her front window. "What is *that* doing here?"

"*That* gave me a ride home. He'll probably leave in a minute."

"Oh, *Baby*! Have the police been harassing you again?"

"No. He just gave me a ride."

She jerked closed the curtains, which happened to be made of Panamanian flags. "This is awful!" she lamented. "If he doesn't leave I'll have to cancel the safe house meeting!"

A half hour later, Mother went out to try to shoo the car away. She returned with her cheeks ablaze. "A free country! I demand an explanation for his intrusive presence on my doorstep, and he tells me it's a free country!"

So Mother was on the phone most of that evening, conferring in heavily accented Spanish with her brood of refugees.

Larry Tchielowicz finally caught me between phone calls. "I've been at the Hall of Justice for the last two hours. Jesus Christ, Willa! What happened to Miles?"

"All I know is, they seem to think I did it!"

My mother, still beside the phone, began gesticulating, something about rocking a baby and putting on a scarf.

"What time did it happen? They kept asking me what I was doing at around eleven. Is that—?"

"What are you doing? No, not you, Larry."

"I still have to call Amanda," my mother fretted. "The Salvadoran lady with the baby, you remember her."

"Well, just a minute. What did you tell them?"

"That there's a police car—"

"Not you, Mother! Larry!"

"I told them I was in class till ten-thirty. Then I went upstairs to talk to Gunnar Haas."

"Gunnar Haas! Why?"

"Baby, I have to call Amanda!"

I motioned for my mother to shush. "What were you talking to him about?"

"Sweden—I might be able to do my tour of duty there. I have to put in my request by—"

"His office is right down the hall from Professor Miles'!"

"I'm aware of that. I went up at around ten thirty-five, ten-forty—"

My mother was anxiously parting the curtains. "I can't let Amanda come here with that Gestapo guard outside! She's not legal."

"I suspected that!"

"What?"

"No, I was talking to my mother. Go ahead."

"Well, Haas got a phone call maybe five minutes after I walked in. He said he had to step out for a second, and he told me to wait in his office. So I sat there and waited."

"Did you hear the shots?"

"Shots!" my mother exclaimed, hastily backing away

from the window. "That policeman isn't shooting anyone, is he?"

I cupped my hand over the mouthpiece and turned toward the wall.

Larry was saying, ". . . window was open, and there was a lot of traffic noise. I thought I heard a car backfire a couple of times. Maybe ten minutes after Haas left. I'm not sure."

My mother came up behind me, startling me into dropping the receiver.

I heard Tchielowicz shout my name, and I picked it back up. "I'm okay. Listen, I'm going to have to go in a minute. But tell me, when did Haas get back to his office?"

"Close to eleven. I don't remember exactly."

"Did he say where he'd been?"

"His nephew's some kind of exchange student. He said he had to go down and vouch for him with security."

"And that took, what, twenty minutes?"

"Apparently he got into it with the guards, said they were harassing the kid because his English isn't good."

"Did he bring this nephew upstairs?"

"Nope."

My mother began yanking on the telephone cord. "Really, Willa! I can't have it on my conscience if they arrest that poor—"

"All right, all right! I've got to go, Larry."

"Pick you up in the morning?"

I barely had time to say yes before Mother wrested the receiver from me.

"You can talk to your friend later, Baby! This is life and death!"

45

By THE TIME Larry picked me up the next morning, my police watchdog had vanished. Larry parked his pea-green tank near Malhousie, and we walked to a closet-sized restaurant around the corner. A hand-lettered sign in the window read: Huasung's Brenkafest Hut.

As we dawdled over spicy eggs and weak coffee, I explained my latest conclusions to Larry. "So the Days wanted to shift the focus of the investigation away from Lady Jane's article and onto the Koenig case."

"I don't get it—why would Jane Day keep an old draft—"

"I've still got the drafts of my *Stanford Daily* articles," I confessed. "You sort of get attached to them. Did you throw out the draft of your tax article?"

"No, but I will now—before you use it to implicate me—"

"Anyway, the Days wanted the cops to waste their time investigating Jake and the connection between his brother-in-law and Susan's aunt. So Day made a partial list of his properties—in green capital letters—and Lady Jane planted it in the filing cabinet.''

''But Nancy Drew, disdaining the help of her inferiors, didn't take the forged will to the police!''

''Good lefties do *not* go to the police, Larry! I'll tell you my war stories some time.''

''I hope not!''

''I don't think Clarence Day and Melissa Whittsen are lovers, after all, though. Not if Day was so anxious to have the police investigate the Koenig thing.'' I picked some red peppers out of my eggs. ''I'd brought up the Koenig case at the dean's cocktail party—I should have known Jane Day was too poised to spill her drink, except on purpose!—and Clarence Day probably thought I knew Melissa was Bonomini's sister. He must have phoned her and asked her to meet him that night. He told me someone had phoned him; I imagine that's what he told Melissa when he got to the restaurant, and what he'd have told the police if I'd been obliging enough to go to them. Gunnar Haas took me to that restaurant because someone had recommended it to him; it must have been Day, gambling that Gunnar would act on the warm recommendation of so august a gentleman.''

Larry frowned at his plate, which had lately contained enough breakfast for a Cambodian village. ''And you really think Mary West was blackmailing the Days?''

''How else could she afford all that expensive leather she's always buying?'' I buried my fingers in my hair, began casing the joint for a cigarette machine.

Larry shook his head. ''Women don't need money.''

''What's that supposed to mean?''

''Every woman I know has a Macy's credit card.'' He

grinned. "You look like a cockatoo when you do that to your hair."

"But look, Mary West edited Susan's article, and she's the only one, besides Henderson and Susan herself, who would have known why Susan didn't cite Jane Day's article."

"That's the flaw in your theory, Nancy Drew. Mary West is a lousy editor. Can you imagine her discovering on her own that Susan hadn't cited a fifteen-year-old source? And Susan would have been crazy to tell Mary anything she wanted kept secret."

We looked at one another across the table. Damn him. He had a point.

46

WE BEAT OUR way through a throng of reporters and security guards to get inside Malhousie; once there, I felt like a woman without a country. The fourth-floor corridor leading to the faculty library and Professor Miles' office had a yellow plastic streamer taped across it. POLICE LINE DO NOT CROSS, it proclaimed. And our old basement office was now a "lounge." The acrylic walls had been torn down, the rug had been scraped off to expose a cement floor, and a dropped-panel ceiling had been erected to hide the plumbing. The battered couches remained, but the desks had been replaced by vending machines full of such delicacies as microwave popcorn.

I didn't feel like socializing, so I preferred that chill, machine-dominated room to the bustling, noisy cafeteria. Few students realized the basement lounge existed, or maybe they stayed away because it reminded them of the murders. When Larry left for his corporate tax class, I had the place to myself.

I put a couple of dimes into a "coffee" machine positioned more or less where my desk used to be. On impulse, I slipped a few quarters into the cigarette machine beside it.

I sank into a sagging couch, wondering what was next. More memorial services? More brownshirts to rough up the neighborhood winos? I remembered a professor at the Christmas cocktail party lamenting that enrollment had declined. Three editors dead: who'd apply to a school where you might get killed if you make law review? "Reverse academic Darwinism," I mused aloud.

"Reverse what?" Harold Scharr dropped down beside me. He slumped there, head thrown back and long legs, in imported navy wool, stretched in front of him. His pale skin throbbed with shadows under his eyes and at his temples.

"Did the police take you to the Hall of Justice yesterday?"

He nodded wearily. "Nice place, if you're a fluorescent light salesman."

"Did they keep you long?"

"Couple of hours." He sat up. "The cops think Ginny was murdered, did you know that? Something about the prints on the gun being wrong. The dean's talking about closing Malhousie down!"

"What!"

"Till fall! Can you believe it? They want to split us up and make us finish out the year at USF and Golden Gate."

"But their classes don't all sync with ours—a lot of people would end up a few credits short of graduating! They wouldn't qualify for the July bar! They'd have to take it in February!"

"And they'd lose the jobs they've worked their tails off to get!" Harold ran a shaky hand through his hair. It was the first time I'd ever seen him mar his appearance. "Listen, Willa, you're the dean's big pet, his sounding board. He's always got you in his office, trying out ideas on you, right?"

"Unfortunately."

He stood up, clasping my hand and tugging me to my feet. "Come up there with me. Right now! Please! Talk to him. Maybe he'll listen to you."

"But—"

"Look, Malhousie's the only law school in Northern California offering labor arbitration this semester. Without those three units I don't graduate!"

Desperation gleamed in his eyes. It's nearly impossible, in these days of government cutbacks, to get a job with the U.S. Attorney. Harold had passed up lucrative summer jobs to clerk for that office, and he'd worked for them twenty hours a week throughout the school year. He'd kept his grades high, written onto law review, and moonlighted as Professor Miles' research assistant, to impress the gov-

ernment with the extra lines on his résumé. But the U.S.
Attorney's office needed litigators; their offer of employment would be promptly rescinded if Harold did not take,
and pass, the July bar exam.

I accompanied him to Dean Sorenson's office.

47

DEAN SORENSON SEEMED distracted, his long hands fid-
geting with the papers on his desk.

"Poor lady," he kept saying of Virginia Miles. "Poor,
dear lady."

His secretary came into the office, wiggling past the
busts of famous lawyers and justices as if expecting wolf
whistles from them. She leaned across the dean's desk,
and a breeze from the open casement windows carried
enough of her Estée Lauder perfume to revive a comatose
ox. "It's time for the memorial and honorarium committee
meeting," she reminded him.

He touched a handkerchief to his damp brow. "My
goodness. Poor lady. We'll establish something. A chair
for trusts scholars, perhaps." He stood up. We followed
suit, but he motioned us to sit back down. "I'll be back

shortly to discuss—what was it? In the meantime, ask Janet to bring you tea or sherry or something.''

Janet gave us a cool smile that warned, Don't you dare. Then she followed the dean out of his office, leaving the door ajar.

Harold frowned at the ring of white plaster busts on curliqued pedestals. ''Justice Hughes was certainly a hirsute fellow,'' he remarked absently.

I fingered the unopened pack of cigarettes on my lap. ''Listen, Harold, yesterday afternoon when they told me I could call a lawyer, I asked for Clarence Day.''

Harold's eyes opened wider. He glanced across the room at the dean's partially open door.

I slid to the edge of my leather chair, letting my voice drop almost to a whisper. I told him about my conversation with Day, including the fine points of my blackmail theory.

He listened, as motionless as the dean's busts.

''Larry doesn't think Mary did it. But I'm sure of it, Harold.''

Harold squinted at the windows flanking the huge desk. Then he shaded his eyes, murmuring, ''It gets more awful every day.''

''Don't you think so? That it must have been Mary?'' How could Larry persist in disbelieving her guilt when it seemed so plain?

''I guess.'' Harold stood up, walking to the bust of Justice Hughes and stroking its plaster beard. ''I don't know.''

I tugged at the cellophane tab of the cigarette pack, opening it with reverent fingers. ''I told Lieutenant Surgelato all this, but he was too mad at me to say anything.''

The acrid smell of unlit tobacco rose from the cigarette pack; I closed my eyes and inhaled greedily.

I could hear Harold pacing behind me. Then he knelt beside my chair. "You're white as a sheet," he observed, putting his hands on my shoulders.

"I'm okay."

He pulled me gently to my feet. "Let's get some air."

"Don't you want to wait for—"

Harold frowned. "Right." Then he glanced at the open windows, his expression brightening. He walked me to the nearest of them, sitting me down on the inner half of the deep ledge.

Then he sat beside me, putting his arm around me. I relaxed my head against the smooth wool of his lapel. The breeze was cool on my neck. It smelled faintly of exhaust from the traffic below.

The dean's office was four stories above Malhousie's delivery entrance. Directly beneath, trash tumbled along the gutter. Three uniformed guards dotted the sidewalk like spilled pennies. There was no sign of reporters; they were probably around front, interviewing the janitor again.

Across the street, derelicts shivered on a grimy brick plaza, waiting for a nearby soup kitchen to open. One of them, slumped against a defunct fountain in his green overcoat and tan fedora, looked like Plead My Case. He seemed to sense me watching him. He yanked off his hat and scanned Malhousie's windows. Then he waved.

I shifted a bit, to face Harold. "Clarence Day's right about one thing," I conceded. "Political careers have survived worse charges than plagiarism."

"It's not exactly the crime of the century." Harold polished a cufflink with his thumb. "But Jane Day's still struggling to get a foot in the door; it wouldn't take much to nip her political career in the bud."

"The blackmail part of my theory is pretty good, don't you think?"

His shrug was noncommittal.

"And Professor Miles being murdered—I mean, my theory accounts for it. Miles is threatening to gossip about Susan's incompetent research, and the only way Susan can keep that from happening is to squeal on Lady Jane. Lady Jane's blackmailer can't risk Lady Jane's 'fessing up and exposing the blackmail. So the blackmailer has to kill one of them—either Susan or Lady Jane—and it makes better business sense to kill Susan."

I broke down and did it; I pulled a cigarette out of the pack. It gave my hand something to do beside crawl into my bangs. "Just think how paranoid you'd be after doing something like that! If anyone mentions Lady Jane's secret to the cops, you're worse off than before. It ties you directly to a murder. And other people who know the secret—you'd start wondering whether to kill them, too. The whole thing could snowball, you know?"

"It could," Harold agreed, glancing down at the top of the guards' caps.

"It has to be Mary West! It has to be an editor—someone who either discovered the secret through research or was taken into Susan's or Henderson's confidence. It has to be someone who loves money enough to blackmail for it, someone with expensive tastes and a small income. And it has to be someone who was right there ready to kill Professor Miles when I made that scene."

I glanced at Harold's handsome profile. His back was

to the window now; he was contemplating the bust of Justice Hughes again.

"And here's the bottom line, Harold. There aren't that many of us left. If Mary didn't do it, who did?"

Harold turned toward me. Not a trace of amicability lingered, not in his eyes, not in his smile.

I blinked, and saw:

Harold Scharr, impeccably dressed in a designer suit; Harold Scharr, with an expensive new sports car I'd heard him put at Hatty McPherson's disposal; Harold Scharr, who as a low-level clerk earned less than a government lawyer. I blinked and saw someone in whom people confided, someone Susan and Henderson would have trusted with a secret. Someone who'd been there to hear my convenient indictment of Professor Miles. Someone clever enough to take advantage of it by choosing that moment to stage her suicide.

Harold must have known Professor Miles had disparaged Susan Green's research—he'd been the professor's assistant. And he'd known Susan well enough to realize she wouldn't stand for it, that she'd sooner expose Jane Day's secret than have her own performance criticized.

And Harold had told me himself about Henderson's Wall Street job offer; he'd known Henderson had lost his incentive to protect Jane Day.

Harold spoke softly. "You might as well."

"Might as well what?"

"Smoke it." He touched my hand with his cold fingertips; I jerked it away, then realized he referred to my cigarette.

Harold frowned, reaching out a long arm to pull a cut-glass lighter off the dean's desk.

He clicked the lighter, and I lit my cigarette, glancing beyond the flame to the dean's door. It was no longer ajar. Harold had closed it when he'd gotten up to examine the rogue's gallery of busts.

I inhaled a searing lungful of smoke, amazed at how sour it tasted. But the nicotine made me brave enough to look out the window.

It was four stories down; the dirty concrete seemed to rush up at me, then plunge back down. A quick push and I'd be nothing but crushed flesh and broken bones.

I took another deep drag and forced myself to look at Harold.

"It was Mary all right," I insisted, hoping my voice didn't betray fear.

I then attempted, with mock casualness, to stand up. Harold grasped my wrist, jerking me back to the stone ledge with a painful jolt to my tailbone.

He looked his old self, his face had relaxed into an amused smile, but he didn't let go of my wrist. "Nice try, Willa. But I have too much respect for your intelligence to believe you haven't figured it out."

An ironic twist to my "you're so smart" fantasy!

I looked out the window again. It was no use screaming; I'd be on the concrete before the guards could help me.

A last cigarette would have been some consolation, but Harold's fingers immobilized my right wrist. My cigarette burned a tantalizing arm's length from my lips. Harold Scharr slid off the ledge, reaching past me to push the casement window fully open. The cold breeze ruffled my hair; I could hear pigeons on the ledge behind me. I hoped for my mother's sake that I didn't take them with me.

I looked up at Harold's perfectly knotted blue tie, at the pressed broadcloth of his shirt, at his thin, pale face and expressive black eyes. "We're alone, Harold—they'll know you did it!"

He shook his head. "You jumped. I came up here with you today so you could confess to the dean."

I did something Nancy Drew would never have done. I called Harold a motherfucker. Then I lunged forward, grabbing at his tie, at his arm, trying to claw my way past him, off the window ledge and into the office.

His hands circled my waist and he lifted me so that my feet were on the slick stone of the outer ledge, scattering pigeons and sliding on their scat. I clutched his narrow shoulder, my hand cold and clumsy with fear. He slid one knee onto the ledge, knocking my left foot out from under me. I struggled to dive over his shoulder, to grab for the window hinge, but Harold rammed his head against my ribs, blocking me, forcing me back. I strained against him, pushing with the one foot I still had on the ledge.

My hand slipped off his shoulder, but I managed to get a fistful of necktie. I clung to it, feeling my right foot slide off the ledge.

I fell hard, my belly still on the window ledge but my legs flailing in space. I tried to pull my knees in, tried to get my feet back on the ledge. Beside me, pigeons squawked and fluttered, deciding to roost elsewhere.

If Harold had pushed me then, pushed me hard enough, I'd have ended up on the concrete. But he paused to disattach my fingers from his necktie.

It was an accident, my using the only weapon I had. I groped along the ledge with my free hand, hoping to find a fingerhold. Instead, I encountered my cigarette. I snatched it up, grinding the lit tip into Harold's cheek.

Swearing, Harold jerked back momentarily, long enough for me to get my knees onto the ledge.

And suddenly there was furious pounding on the dean's door. Someone was shouting, "Security! Open up!"

Harold went rigid with shock, and I pulled myself past him, off the ledge. I stumbled over his foot, ending up on my belly again, this time at Harold's feet. I lay there panting for a moment, listening to the brownshirts batter the door.

Then I scooted away, wheezing, "Give up, Harold! It's over!"

But Harold did not agree. He dropped to his knees, his face flushed and his eyes round with frenzy. He knotted his fingers into my sweater.

The pounding grew louder, and I heard myself whisper, "Come *on*, fascists!"

He half lifted, half pushed me back toward the ledge, his strength astonishing me. My shoulders slammed against the inner margin, knocking the breath out of me. Harold scrambled to his feet, trying to hoist me over.

And then the pounding stopped.

Harold stopped, too, turning his face toward the door. The sound of a key in the lock was as loud and as beautiful a sound as I've ever heard.

The color drained from Harold's face. He released my sweater and straightened up, shrugging his suit jacket back into proper alignment, tucking in his tie.

Then he looked down at me, and touched the small cigarette burn on his cheek. "How could you?" he reproached me.

48

PLEAD MY CASE had saved my life. He'd recognized me sitting on the window ledge, just as I'd recognized him sprawled beside the plaza fountain. A person of unimpaired mental function might have seen me up there and thought nothing of it. But no prudent wino (relatively speaking) would dream of perching in a fourth-floor window; and Plead My Case saw no reason to assume my balance was any better than his. Since I'd provided him with many dollars' worth of liquid warmth over the years, he decided to bestir himself on my behalf. He wove his way across the street and accosted the security guards. If he'd mentioned the dean's window to them at the outset, the guards would have looked up and seen me sitting serenely, in no danger of falling. Instead, Plead My Case got sidetracked and began ranting about taxes, of all things. Just as the guards decided to haul him away to the drunk tank, he remembered his errand and pointed to the dean's window. One of the guards glanced up, not because he understood Plead My Case, but because it's human nature to look at something when somebody points to it.

And the guard saw me struggling with Harold Scharr.

The federal income tax system may have undermined my grade point average, but had it been any less Byzantine, it might not have obsessed the old wino. And if Plead My Case hadn't wasted a few crucial moments raving about it, I'd have fallen right off the tax rolls.

As it was, the guard radioed other guards posted near the faculty library. They dashed to the dean's office and began pounding on the door, which Harold had locked by depressing a little button on the knob.

When the police moseyed upstairs a few minutes later to continue investigating Professor Miles' murder, they found a corridor full of security guards in macho delirium over having caught a murderer.

By the time Surgelato joined them, the dean's secretary's tiny antechamber was crammed full of excited men. I sat in a corner, watching the police advise Harold of his rights. In spite of myself, I felt a greater kinship with him than I did with the loud, sweating men who'd rescued me from him.

Surgelato watched me watch Harold, then he put his arm around me and steered me out of the room.

In the elevator, I asked him, "Did you know it was Harold?"

I'd met enough Italians to understand his "but of course" gesture. "Nothing we could pull him in for, but we had our suspicions. The nice clothes, the car—too much cash, no debts. It was the only thing made any of you stand out, really. Criminal records, a couple of you.'' He smiled at me. ''Judge Rondi gave you two months back in 1971.''

''Judge Rondi is a fascist.''

''I spent that long in the hospital back then. Brick in the head.''

''I got night-sticked—''

''Okay, okay. Point is, we were looking at now, not then.''

The elevator doors opened, and Surgelato escorted me through a lobby and patio full of nattering reporters. He handed me into a marked police car, shielding the open door with his body.

As he straightened up, I asked him a final question. ''Lieutenant, who called security?'' I had yet to read the details in Manuel Boyd's article about Plead My Case.

''Old wino hangs around here.''

''I'll be damned! Next time you're in trouble—''

He smiled, slamming the door. ''Sure, call a wino.''

49

Six hours later, I located Larry Tchielowicz on the library's mezzanine balcony. He was sitting crankily in a carrel near the staircase.

He leaped to his feet when he saw me, grabbing my arm and pulling me downstairs to a gloomy, cinderblock cavern of a landing.

"Harold Scharr! Jesus!" His close-set eyes glittered, whether with anger or distress, I couldn't say. "Reporters have been going ape-shit! They had to triple security to keep them out of here! Have you seen the headlines?"

I leaned against the cold cement. It had been an adventure, beating my way through the reporters. I wouldn't have bothered, but I seemed to be in love.

"Are you okay? What happened exactly?"

When Tchielowicz learned how close the timing had been, he almost crushed me. I hoped that he'd kiss me, but he didn't. I wasn't sure what to do about it.

"Is it the herpes?"

"Willa!"

"I *have* been around. That used to be considered quite

225

normal." Depressing to think of myself as an aging, herpetic hippie, defending the sexual revolution.

"Oh, Willa, look—I was out of line that day. What I said about Jake and Professor Haas, that was—"

"I don't want an apology! I want—"

"Let me lay this to rest. I didn't want to tell you about"—he looked away, addressing a cinderblock wall—"you know, what I went to jail for. I didn't tell you because— People tend to treat me differently when they find out."

"Larry, I've known for months. I did some checking. I found out all about it."

He stepped away from me.

I didn't know what else to do. I kept talking. "I got that anonymous note. I found out Henderson had called your orphanage. I suppose he was checking up on everybody. He'd been blackmailing Gunnar Haas—maybe he was afraid Gunnar would tell the police. Maybe he was looking for some mud to sling at us, just in case. Anyway, the note was probably an anal little memo to himself. He probably just stuck it away in his desk. And you can guess what happened to it there. Greg Parker took it! After Henderson died, Greg must have felt like he should do something with the note. So he left it on my desk and— Jesus, Larry! Say something!"

"I don't know what to say. How do you feel about it?"

"I told you—I've known for months. I haven't treated you any differently, have I?"

His smile was tentative. "I'm back in uniform a month after the bar exam."

"I could get Julian Warneke to give me that month off— Larry! If you wanted me to!"

I don't think he came to me, I think I went to him.

Footsteps echoed in the stair beneath the landing. Pinball morons, as loud as a herd of buffalo.

One was saying, *"Law School, Part Four: Harold Lives!"* The others guffawed.

Tchielowicz stopped kissing me.

He drew me into the corner, speaking quietly as they clamored past. "I might eventually get assigned to the Presidio. It'll be anywhere from Europe to Oklahoma till then. But air fare's not bad. You'd have vacations, and I'd have leave."

"You might even get court-martialed."

"We can always hope!" he said dryly.

50

THE NEXT MORNING, Jane and Clarence Day were arrested for Greg Parker's murder. I was in bed all that day, so I missed the brouhaha. I later saw news footage of them being led from a police car to the Hall of Justice, though, and I have to give them credit: they nodded pleasantly and waved, just like the Prince and Princess of Wales.

The police found the parcel of stolen law review articles in the trunk of Harold Scharr's sports car. Clever Harold, he knew I'd suspect Professor Miles of the mischief. He waited for me to accuse her, then he spirited me away to allow the professor time to complain to the dean.

Five minutes after leaving me in the café, Harold dispatched Virginia Miles. From her office, he telephoned the police about a "theft." He knew the police would hear the saga of the law review articles from the dean; they could consider it a motive for suicide or murder, as they chose.

By the time the police released those stolen articles, the summer issue had become ludicrously dated. I was out of law school by then, though, and I didn't much care. I was visiting Larry in Lawton, Oklahoma, the flattest, ugliest town in the known universe.

That belated summer issue was the last to identify Gunnar Haas as faculty advisor. Gunnar returned to Sweden, fearing that his minor role in the drama (succumbing to Henderson's blackmail) would be made public, and that the dean would ask for his resignation. Poor Gunnar. I talked to him for a few minutes before he left, and he wouldn't meet my eye. Instead he chatted about his young nephew, who was an exchange student in San Francisco and who would be accompanying him back to Sweden. It turned out that I had met young Piers, pronounced "Parse" by everyone except his sponsor, Jane Day, who persisted in calling him "Pierce."

I ran into Hatty McPherson outside Gunnar's office. She confided to me that Gunnar was taking her out for a "discrete dinner." She said the two of them had shared many such dinners in her three years at Malhousie. She wondered if he'd write to her in New York; she'd been hired by Wailes, Roth, Fotheringham & Beck.

The last time I saw Mary West she was as big as a barn. She said she'd be raising the baby alone, but she didn't seem overly concerned. "It'll be easy raising a kid on a lawyer's salary."

"Where are you going to be working?"

There was a twinkle of malice in her eye. "Me? I'll be at home with Junior. It's Jake's salary I'm talking about."

Jake Whittsen went back to Alaska when classes ended in May. He and Melissa reconciled, apparently deciding to overlook their respective affairs.

I imagine Melissa's former lover viewed the reconciliation with regret, but Martin Relke, Larry's roommate, would have little trouble finding himself a chipmunky Mills coed to replace her. I seemed to be the only woman in Northern California who found his Aryan countenance repulsive.

I was furious with Larry for not having told me it was Martin whom Melissa had been seeing. Larry shrugged. "It wasn't my secret."

"You could at least have told me it wasn't Clarence Day in the picture with Melissa!"

"Me and Relke had this little party. Melissa was there—she told Jake she was going out of town. And Judy—remember her?"

"With the kneesocks?"

"She had a new camera; she took a whole bunch of pictures. Next morning, she brought them to the law review office, started showing them to me." He grinned. "She was sitting in Greg Parker's chair, by the way."

"I knew it!"

"And of all the rotten luck, who walks in but Whittsen! He gets a book out of the bookcase, looks down at Judy, and sees her holding a photograph—of his wife wrapped around Relke!"

"Where did a Nazi youth like Relke meet someone as classy as Melissa, anyway?"

"Jake took her to a Republican League dinner."

"Jake Whittsen is a *Republican*?"

Larry laughed. "You didn't look half as disgusted when you thought he was a murderer!"